DEVIL'S CLAW

DEVIL'S CLAW
By Valerie Davisson
Copyright © 2019 Valerie Davisson

Published by Vaughn House Publishing, Depoe Bay, OR
Second Edition
Previously Published by Hauser Publishing in 2016
Print ISBN - 978-0-9838696-6-5
Ebook ISBN - 978-0-9838696-7-2

Cover and Interior Design by Kimberly Peticolas, www.kimpeticolas.com

Library of Congress Control Number: 2019912517

10   9   8   7   6   5   4   3   2   1

DEVIL'S CLAW

A Logan McKenna Novel

VALERIE DAVISSON

To Mom, for instilling in me a love of books, ideas, and the natural world—and for your strength, independence, and resilience.

Prologue

The man pushed himself back from his drafting table, rose slowly, and walked to the window. His right knee protested, but he shook it out to make it pop. The tall stool continued to spin for a few seconds before settling down. Normally the work came easily, but not today.

Maybe I'm just getting old.

Perched halfway up one of the steepest canyons in Jasper, California, he could see for miles up and down the coast, the spectacular view interrupted only by Devil's Claw, an ancient rock formation defining the north end of Main Beach. Layers of basalt, upended by tectonic forces and eroded over time, created the massive, aptly named landmark, reaching out into the Pacific toward Pelican Island a few miles offshore. It had been Solange's favorite place.

Memorizing the tide tables, his fifteen-year-old daughter quickly learned exactly when the sea's presents would arrive. Bundled in one of his old sweatshirts, the teenager could often be found sitting quietly on one of Devil's knobby stone knuckles, sketchbook in hand, capturing on paper whatever sea life was momentarily caught in its grip. Occasionally, she spotted her favorite subject, the sea otter, popping its sleek head up beyond the breakers or even closer in, floating on its back, cracking an abalone shell open on its stomach.

She could sit for hours, just looking out to sea. He never asked what she was thinking, but he assumed it was often about her mother. On the days she spent at the beach, she cried less, and that, too, he assumed was good.

Back in the studio, he helped her turn these first, amateurish renderings of sea stars, octopuses, anemones, and crabs into surprisingly good clay and wire sculptures. Like he, she thought in 3-D. He encouraged his daughter's training and freely supplied extra materials to the cause.

Those were good years. Unsure what to do after his wife, Marie, died, he moved them back here, back home. It had been good for them both.

Marie.

Unbidden, the smell of her perfume floated past. Tahitian Ginger. In 1942, still in art school, it wasn't exactly in his budget, but he made sure she had it. Perfume, not cologne.

The man smiled.

Furious, Marie's father refused to speak to him when he learned of their marriage, but her mother was pleased. Like most French people, she liked Americans, but Monsieur Moreau made it clear he did not. He had nothing against Americans per se, but was very protective of his daughter.

"He is a soldier, and like all soldiers, he will leave."

But Robert didn't leave. He'd surprised the old man, and himself, by not getting on the military transport that morning or any others leaving later that week. Of vague French ancestry himself and an artist, Robert Sauvage felt more at home in

Paris than in the States. Restless, with a rebellious streak, he also enjoyed defying parents on both sides of the Atlantic. After art school, he quickly established a successful career as a sculptor. They lived well.

Marie made sure their daughter was raised properly, keeping her well away from his seedier artist friends. Solange attended if not the best schools, then the best schools they could afford. Uniforms were de rigueur for students during the day, but her mother indulged her daughter's desire for color, texture, and line with a wardrobe any Hollywood star would envy. Marie considered clothing an acceptable outlet for a girl's artistic tendencies versus the very male, physical profession of sculpting.

After Marie died, Paris was no longer the city of lights, at least not for Robert. A few months later, when news reached him of his mother's passing—his father had died a few years before—he returned home to settle their affairs.

Once there, he decided to stay. Solange needed a change. Of course, fifteen-year-olds are moody anyway, but he thought it would be good for her to be away from her still-grieving grandparents and the large, darkened rooms of their Paris apartment. It certainly would be good for him. Marie's father somehow blamed him for her death. As if he'd had anything to do with it. She succumbed to the flu. Quickly, and to the surprise of them all. Other than smoking, which typified all Parisians, Marie had no other vices and had always been healthy.

California suited him. Tangy sea air tinged with the sharp scent of sage; the vast, empty Pacific; and a sky so blue it hurt. After years of Parisian life, the relatively untamed West Coast felt as exotic to him as Paris had in his twenties. In Paris, nothing was natural. In California, everything was.

Here, he could become himself.

Though still undeveloped compared to the suburban sprawl inland, the tiny coastal town of Jasper had become a thriving artists' colony in his absence. He began to work before they'd even unpacked. Vigorous and fresh, his new pieces sold well. He even picked up some parcels of raw land. On one of them, up in the canyon, with its panoramic views, he built this private aerie, flooded with natural light. Once settled in his studio, he largely ignored the other properties although some of them were much more valuable. They were also much closer to people, and he needed space and quiet to work.

Free from her mother's constraints, Solange happily assisted in the studio, soaking up all Robert could teach, but soon outgrew him and their insular world. At eighteen, she applied to and was accepted by his old art school in Paris. Suitcase in hand, she left on her nineteenth birthday.

And didn't look back.

He was surprised how much this bothered him at first, but he couldn't hold it against her. Like father, like daughter. He had lived his life. Why shouldn't she live hers? It wasn't her job to keep him company and care for him in his old age.

And he wasn't alone for long. There was Janet. One minute, she was in his studio; the next, she was in his bed. He still wasn't sure exactly how that had happened. Nothing like Marie, of course, but Janet fit nicely into his life. Cheerful, uncomplicated, and so very young. Not her fault. She easily morphed into running his household and his business, allowing him the freedom he craved. They were together almost six, no, seven years.

Robert didn't agonize over decisions. He just knew he needed to make one. Now.

The soothing sound of breaking waves and seagull cries reached his ears. A solitary surfer caught a wave, riding it briefly to shore.

He turned back to his desk, where dust motes, suspended in the afternoon light, hovered over the unfinished letter.

It was the right thing to do. The least he could do.

He picked up his pen.

Dear Janet . . .

He had no idea this one simple act, hidden for years, would erupt into a vicious battle, threatening those he loved, eventually crushing the life of an innocent.

1

SATURDAY, JUNE 20, 2015

Crunching gravel as quietly as she could, Logan backed Lola out of the driveway and rolled past still-sleeping neighbors toward the light at the bottom of Killer Hill. They were both looking forward to an early morning cruise down Pacific Coast Highway, before it became clogged with tourist traffic. Other than a recording session this afternoon with a couple of her student leaders, Logan had two glorious days off until Monday and planned to enjoy them.

A graduation gift from Logan's father, Lola was Logan's '58 Corvette. The sapphire beauty with white leather interior gleamed inside and out, thanks to the loving attentions of Mr. Delgado, mechanic extraordinaire. He left the chrome scoops Logan loved on the sides but discretely took out extra weight and put in extra power, making Lola a very fit female of a certain age. And in Southern California, that was saying something. Nothing made Lola happier than flying effortlessly over miles of empty highway, flirting with her pal, the Pacific.

June gloom was still in effect, but as far as Logan was concerned, every day was a top-down day, sun or no sun. By the time she reached San Juan Capistrano, half of her hair had escaped the baseball cap she'd jammed on her head this morning. She didn't mind a bit. She wasn't as particular about her looks as Lola was.

Two hours later, energized by the drive, she couldn't wait to tackle the kitchen. Not that it needed much in the way of spring cleaning; she barely used it. Logan only used her oven for one thing—her signature dish—roast chicken. Her foreign-exchange mom made sure she learned to cook at least one French basic well. Stuffed with lemons and rosemary sprigs, basted in butter, it came out perfect every time and made her compact beach bungalow smell heavenly.

After a brief stop at the local market for supplies, she parked in the driveway, between the house and what used to be the garage. It was now the studio where she was to meet the boys at 1:00 p.m.

Keys in hand, she headed for the front door. Morning glories tangled along the fence, shielding house from street. French thyme nicely filled in the spaces between the slate paving stones, creating the meandering walkway. On damp mornings, she purposely stepped between the pavers so the herbs would release their pungent, savory aroma.

She recently painted the front door a bright, blue-green color. Bonnie called it seafoam green. Logan had no idea. She just liked it. It reminded her of mermaids.

Once inside, she hung her keys and purse on one of the heavy-duty hooks just inside the door and carried the groceries and cleaning supplies into the kitchen.

Normally, her tiny, domed fridge was stocked only with Logan's idea of essentials—real butter and a good char-donnay—but for tonight's barbecue with Ben, she'd added fresh salad makings and a bowl of just-picked strawberries. Next, she refilled the miniature ice trays—no automatic ice maker in this vintage model. She knew she should upgrade the appliances, but she loved the vintage look of them, and it made her feel connected to the original owner of the house, Meg, an eccentric writer who died in her eighties. Logan never met her, but from everything she'd heard about her, they would have hit it off.

One of Jean's freshly baked baguettes from Tava'e's down the hill rested aromatically on the counter, in a basket Bonnie had given her. Food-wise, she was good to go. Ben usually provided anything that actually had to be cooked. He was the chef; Logan was more of an assembler.

Being in a relationship, particularly with a next-door neighbor, was not something Logan had planned when she bought her fixer-upper two years ago, but the last few years had been anything but predictable.

Last summer, with the help of his crew on their off hours, Ben had helped Logan convert her garage into a recording studio and added an upstairs office. Killer Hill was steep, so even with the addition, she didn't lose the view from her rooftop deck. Lola, however, still hadn't forgiven Logan for commandeering her garage. She'd have to make it up to her this summer with a nice detail and tune-up at Mr. Delgado's.

Ben, nicknamed the Viking by her best friend, Bonnie, had been there with her as she rebuilt every aspect of her life. In fact, he and Purgatory probably saved her life two summers ago when a deranged woman with a very large knife attacked her in her bed. Declared incapable of standing trial, the young woman was currently locked away in a hospital for the criminally insane, many miles away.

Everyone liked Ben. He'd even passed inspection with her little brother, Rick, a police officer. It didn't hurt that Ben's dog, Purgatory, and Rick's K-9 partner, a German shepherd named Charlie, had a thing going, too. BBQs were a regular lovefest.

Last summer, Ben and Logan exorcised enough of their own personal demons to realize their friendship was turning into love. The last ten months had been better than she could have imagined, but for now, she wasn't ready for more.

Her current life seemed light-years away from her life with Jack.

Four years ago, she and her husband ran a successful computer business they built from scratch, and their daughter, Amy, had recently graduated from UC San Diego and was off in Africa doing research.

Then came the car accident that changed everything. It took her husband's life and left Logan with humbling back and neck injuries. During her painful physical recovery, she also dealt with the discovery that Jack had been unfaithful during much of their marriage. Her old life shattered, she'd been forced to contemplate a new one. It hadn't been easy.

That first year could only be described as a deep, black hole of depression sprinkled with anxiety attacks. The daily struggle almost undid her. At some point, though, she realized she wanted to live, not just exist.

She still wasn't sure what her new life would look like in the end, but she knew she wanted to find out.

Cleaning the entire downstairs took all of thirty minutes. Barefoot, she couldn't do her signature sock slide on the refinished hardwood floors, but she smiled at the thought of it. Bella, her violin, handed down from her paternal grandmother, took pride of place on the living room wall.

Checking the time again, she put away her meager cleaning supplies and hoped the boys were on schedule for their session.

She wanted time to shower and get ready for her evening with Ben. A landscape architect, he was doing some work in town today but said he'd be there by five thirty.

When she was growing up, music had been a central part of Logan's world. In high school, she played fiddle in a bluegrass band and at the local arts festival with her friends Ned and Sally. When Amy was born, it was obvious she had inherited the family love of music. A true McKenna, Amy danced before she could walk, whirling with joyful abandon to the Appalachian clogging tunes.

Jack always felt left out. He didn't play an instrument and wasn't particularly interested in being the audience. He wanted his wife and daughter at his rugby games. Gradually, as Jack and the business took more and more of her time, her violin and her music got pushed literally and figuratively to the back of her closet.

Playing again was like opening a window in a stuffy room.

Leaving the French doors open, she checked the clock. 12:55 p.m. Grabbing her violin, she slipped on some flip-flops she kept near the door and made her way around the back, past the stairs leading up to the deck. She arrived just as the boys were getting out of Brandon's car.

"Hi, Ms. McKenna!" Brandon yelled.

"Hello, Mrs. McKenna," Jeff said.

Brandon reached into the back seat of his Kia to lift out a beat-up guitar case. Plastered in travel and surf stickers, it was a hand-me-down from his dad, a local musician and former member of a semi-famous rock group, Bone Temple. They broke up in the '80s over girls and drugs. *Qu'est* surprise.

"Hi, guys," Logan said, pulling a key out of her pocket.

Unlocking a small door, she entered the cool interior of her former garage and switched on a light. The door to the sound studio was straight ahead. Directly to her left, narrow, steep stairs led up to the large, open office area from which she ran her music/math program, Fractals. They still hadn't installed a safety railing. It was on the list. As she learned when fixing up her house, remodels were never finished.

The boys followed her inside, everyone's eyes taking a minute to adjust to the darker interior.

"You get any surf time in?" Logan asked, opening the studio door with her free hand.

"Yeah, waves were a little flat, but we got in some good rides," Brandon said, coming in behind her, taking his guitar out of its case on a small table just inside the door. Jeff nodded. A part-time lifeguard, Brandon could always be found in or near the ocean. Friends since the third grade, Jeff went where Brandon went, and Ben's nephews thought both boys were cool.

Although best friends, in every other way, they were a study in contrasts. Brandon's wavy hair, bleached white and stiff with saltwater, stuck out from a friendly, sunburned face. The sun had no effect on Jeff's hair. It remained completely black, shiny and stick straight, no matter how much time he spent in the water. As always, his bangs needed to be cut. Jeff was the quiet one.

The first two student leaders Logan selected, both boys worked hard and really helped get *Fractals* off the ground its first year. Now in high school, they'd been in Logan's seventh grade class the one year she worked in the classroom. The boys' pick for the program's new name, Fractals, was inspired by one of Logan's math lessons. Even though fractals weren't part of the regular geometry curriculum, Logan hadn't exactly been a regular teacher. The students had been awed by how fractals not only created beautiful, kaleidoscope graphics, but were patterns underlying everything in the universe, including math and music, on any scale, and were created with a very simple equation.

"I love it!" Mrs. Houser said when told of the new name, just before writing a check, so *Fractals* it was.

Logan didn't know where the woman got her money, but she was just happy Mrs. Houser was willing to part with some of it.

Even with her benefactor's generous checkbook, Logan was always searching for ways to pay for instruments, equipment, software licenses, and just office supplies. Today's pizza was coming out of her pocket. These guys could easily put away a large meat lover's each.

Since Logan had loaned her fiddling efforts to the first recordings, they begged her to play on their current project. She agreed only if they kept the profits for themselves. College was only two short years away for these boys, and she knew they'd need every penny, no matter who got into the White House. Campaign promises of free tuition for every child were just that . . . promises.

Although finding time in her schedule was tough, Logan loved these sessions. Getting away from the mound of paperwork on her desk and putting off dealing with district pencil pushers whose only vocabulary word seemed to be *no*, even for a few hours, was glorious.

As musicians, Brandon and Jeff were developing in skill and range, but it was Jeff's voice and songwriting that really set him apart. His strong vocals and tongue-in-cheek lyrics captured your attention. The resulting sound reminded Logan of a cross between Keb' Mo' and Ben Harper. The boy was truly talented.

Though 4:00 p.m. came all too soon, they got a few good tracks down before they wrapped it up. Jeff's shift at Athena's, one of the food court restaurants in the Otter Festival, started at four thirty. He only worked three days a week. To avoid paying benefits, most places didn't give kids more than twenty hours. Brandon was going home to watch a Star Wars marathon. His lifeguard hours were usually early in the morning.

Locking the studio behind them, Logan walked the boys out to their truck. The sun was still out, but lower in the sky and not as strong. Logan's large tortoiseshell cat, Dimebox, emerged from the long shadow of the hedge separating her property from the next house down the hill. It was a fixer-upper like hers, and the young couple who bought it were racing to finish the remodel before their baby arrived, which, by the look of the wife, could be any day now. Winding around the boys' feet, rubbing against their legs, Dimebox pressed for a scratch behind the ears. Jeff was happy to oblige. His mom was allergic, so they didn't have pets.

Named after a small town in Texas "no bigger'n a dime box worth of snuff," Dimebox weighed in at fourteen pounds and was the king of all he surveyed. He didn't start out that way. When Logan first scooped up the flea-infested, scrawny kitten, he fit into the crook of her arm.

"What time do you want us back on Monday?" Brandon asked.

"Same time works for me," Logan said. "If I don't hear you when you get here, yell up at the window. I'll be in the office."

Jeff said that worked for him, too.

Violin tucked under her arm, she waved at their taillights and Brandon's outstretched arm and checked her watch.

Almost Ben time!

Deciding to catch the sunset while she waited for Ben on the rooftop deck, Logan went inside and quickly assembled her supplies into a canvas bag. Bottle of pinot noir. Two glasses. Some crackers and cheese. Adjusting it onto her shoulder, she left the doors open and went up the outside stairs.

14

The rooftop deck had been one of the major selling points of this house.

After paying off the debts she didn't know Jack had accumulated, the cash purchase and remodel of the house took every cent she had. But she'd been determined to own her own home. A lifelong renter, she still got a thrill from coming home to *her* house. *And* she loved not having a house payment.

The deck was Logan's escape hatch, a place where she could close her eyes and just listen to the waves or marvel at the many changing colors of the Pacific. She tried to name them once, but Mother Nature's palette quickly outran her vocabulary.

Dimebox trotted up behind her. Ever loyal to her for rescuing him from the pound, he guarded his mistress and faithfully brought her presents of mice, small birds, and moles.

She found another one of his grisly gifts this morning on the back porch.

Well, like her father always said, it was the thought that counted.

2

THURSDAY, JULY 2, 2015, 3:17 A.M.

Inky black, the satin surface of the Pacific stretched west, away from the solitary swimmer, toward an empty horizon. A few miles east, to her right, lay the barely visible outline of the ghostly gray shore. Libra, faint through the coastal clouds, held the scales of justice and harmony overhead.

Floating on her back, she seemed unconcerned about being separated from her colony, alone and without protection. The ocean was her home. For a few hours, she continued to float in the open water, drifting in and out of sleep. She needed her rest; she had just given birth.

A three-pound ball of fluff lay on the mother's chest. Eyes not yet open, she knew only the warmth and security of her mother's body and its steady stream of nourishing milk.

Neither of them saw the fin. Approaching silently from the open sea, the shark lunged. Sharp, serrated teeth easily pierced the mother's thick fur, just missing her spine. Powerful jaws lifted her out of the water, then, just as quickly, realizing she wasn't a fat, juicy seal, spit her back out.

It was over in less than a minute.

Incredibly, the pup managed to hang on during the attack, and as the shark swam away, she got back to the business of living. For all she knew, this was a normal event. Maybe the next second would bring death. But for now, the water, which, seconds ago, had been a froth of bloody violence, lay calm, so she again latched on to her mother's breast.

While her pup nursed contentedly, the new mother weakly paddled. Using the last of her energy, she nuzzled her baby's head, holding it between her paws to keep her from falling into the sea.

An hour later, left leg useless now, she couldn't paddle at all. A thin ribbon of warm blood trailed behind her as the current carried them closer to the shore.

3

THURSDAY, JULY 2, 2015, 6:15 A.M.

Logan knew Amy would probably still be in bed. Although she was normally an early riser, the medicine made her sleepy.

Home from Africa after a bout of malaria, she was staying with Liam in a rental cottage he found only a few bocks away. The doctor said she'd be okay, just needed lots of rest and a regular schedule to regain her strength. Logan was impressed with the way Liam took care of everything seamlessly.

Locking the door behind her, Logan zipped her hoodie halfway up and started walking down the hill. Cool mornings were one of the perks of living at the beach.

Might as well pick up some breakfast. Tava'e's was on the way, at the bottom of her street. Named for its homicidal effect on manual transmissions, Killer Hill kept most cars and bikes to streets with lesser inclines. Another benefit of living here, as far as Logan was concerned.

Amy was as addicted to cinnamon rolls as Logan was. She

wondered if Liam was a health-food nut or if he would enjoy one, too. She and Ben had met him last Thanksgiving but really didn't know that much about him.

When Logan walked into the bakery, a booming voice greeted her from the back.

"Talofa!"

Tava'e, as always this time of day, was holding court in her booth, beating someone at chess.

Without interrupting her game but still acknowledging her greeting, Logan made her way over to the booth to say a quick hello before ordering Amy's breakfast to go. By the time she got there, though, the graceful monolith was already up, crushing her in a hug. Being enveloped in a Tava'e hug made you feel safe from all harm.

"It is good to see you," Tava'e said as she sat back down. "How is your daughter?" she added, indicating Logan should take her companion's place.

"She was just about to beat me, anyway," Tava'e's former competitor said, graciously giving up his seat.

"Epiphany! Two cinnamon rolls, one to go . . . ," Tava'e said.

A much-pierced barista with indigo octopus tentacles caressing her neck materialized at her side. Logan noticed she'd removed her eyebrow ring since she last saw her but had added ebony earplugs.

Epiphany placed a huge cinnamon roll slathered in vanil-la-bean frosting on a plain white plate in front of Logan, along with a large cup of black coffee, then handed her a small but bulging paper sack. The coffee came in a thick, wide mug, complete with saucer. No paper cups inside. Those were only available in the to-go line.

"Hi, Logan. Here are your rolls. I put an extra one in for Amy's Scottish guy."

As if Amy kept a collection of foreign men, making it necessary to specify nationality.

"How does she do that?" Logan asked. "I didn't even order yet!"

Tava'e laughed. "I just hope she never quits. I couldn't find anyone half as good at this job, and Danny would be lost without her."

A few minutes later, sated and caffeinated, outside on the sidewalk, Logan pushed the "Walk" button at the intersection.

Hopefully Amy was up, They needed to get going while it was still cool. The morning haze was already burning off, and the doctor said she shouldn't overdo it.

7:27 a.m.

"Mom! Mom!"

Amy ran down the beach. Against doctor's orders, of course. She was only supposed to start with mild exercise, which is what this morning's walk was supposed to be—a short stroll down to Devil's Claw to explore the tide pools.

Logan ran to catch up.

Amy was pointing to a large, tangled clump of seaweed. The retreating tide threatened to carry it back out.

"Get that end!" Amy shouted.

Logan grabbed one of the slippery dark-green strands at the top and helped pull the heavy bundle farther up on the sand. Whatever was caught in the seaweed wasn't moving and was attracting flies. It couldn't have been there long, or the crabs would have been all over it.

She hoped Amy wouldn't be too upset when it turned out to be one of the dead seals that sometimes washed up on the beach overnight. It was upsetting to see one, but as Logan had learned growing up in a beach town, not that uncommon.

She'd seen dead seals before, even a baby gray whale once.

"Don't touch it, hon," Logan said, pulling out her phone with her other hand. They'd have to call animal control.

"Mom! It's moving! There are two of them. Look! It's a baby! A baby sea otter!"

Amy was right. On closer inspection, Logan saw the telltale thick brown pelt identifying the larger, obviously dead, animal as a sea otter. The sodden bump of light-brown fur lying on top must be her pup.

Logan remembered reading someplace that unlike seals, protected by layers of blubber, sea otters only had their fur to keep them warm. Mothers had to constantly groom the babies and teach them to roll frequently in the water in order to help hold insulating air bubbles in their coats.

Matted and out of water, this little pup was in trouble.

After instructing Amy to shelter the tiny survivor from the searing rays of the sun, Logan pulled out her phone and dialed 411. The sun, of course, had decided to make its appearance early today. There wasn't a shred of marine layer left to shelter the little guy.

She remembered the name of a facility from a fund-raising brochure near the register at Tava'e's, stacked next to some real estate flyers: Southern Sea Otter Sanctuary and Education Center. When 411 found the number, they connected her call. She waited impatiently while the phone rang.

Someone answered, but she couldn't hear them clearly over the sound of the waves. She walked a little farther up the sand.

"Hello, is this the sea otter center?"

"Yes, this is the Southern Sea Otter Sanctuary and Education Center," a woman replied. "We're not open yet, but you have the right number. How can I help you?

"I'm not sure if you can help if you're not open yet, but my daughter and I found a dead sea otter, and . . ."

"A sea otter? Are you sure?"

"Yes, pretty sure. It's definitely not a seal. I've seen those. And this animal has what looks like a newborn pup on her. It's breathing, but just barely," Logan said, adding, "Open or not, I think you've got your first customer."

After giving the woman, who turned out to be the director of the center, their location, all Logan and Amy could do was wait for the cavalry to arrive. Their main job, per the director's strict instructions, was to keep aggressive seagulls, dogs, and curious beachgoers at bay.

Logan looked again. So far, the pup was still alive. She hoped it stayed that way.

Crouching down, Logan attempted to clear some of the seaweed away without disturbing the pup. Lifting one of the larger strands, she could see the mother's side had a big gash in it. Not good.

Although still rare, there'd been more otter sightings lately: one in Huntington Beach and one off Catalina Island. But they had all been solitary males. She wondered what made this otter, a female and a new mother, venture this far south alone.

4

Only three miles south as the crow flies, the rocky fingers of Devil's Claw reached across the beach toward Bird Island and prevented Gina Richards from driving directly from the center to the injured sea otter. The Wrangler could handle sand but wasn't up to climbing rocks. She'd have to take the highway up and around, then double back.

Every second she lost in traffic was agonizing. Previously employed by the Monterey Bay Aquarium, she had been called out to many of these otter strandings before and knew time was of the essence.

As she pulled onto the highway, she reached under the front seat and pressed the bar to adjust the seat position to long and tall. Much better. Dennis drove it last.

At five seven, her new assistant, twenty-seven-year-old Dennis Radmore, usually drove his own vehicle, but right now, he was driving on bald tires, so she insisted he take the Jeep to do errands during work hours. He was one of her best citizen scientists up in Monterey, so she brought Dennis down as soon as possible after she took the job here. Dedicated, knowledgeable, and easy to work with, he was the first and, for now, the only hire until the rest of the certification process was complete.

Due to her expertise and experience, most of the approvals had been granted, but there were a few more desks to clear before they were deemed prepared to accept injured sea otters and could officially open.

Adjusting the rearview mirror, she caught a glimpse of herself: short dark curls, shot with silver, blew up against the rim of a floppy canvas hat. She was fair skinned and apple cheeked, and the tip of her small nose was perpetually pink and in some stage of peeling.

Hoping she had everything else she needed, Gina picked up speed. The Jeep responded nicely. Solange wanted her to buy the Land Rover. Electric everything, leather, GPS, and back-up viewer. But Gina insisted on the stripped-down Wrangler.

"Marine-mammal vets don't need a leather interior to haul injured animals and equipment," she had explained.

Fewer features also meant fewer things to break, and the fifteen thousand dollars they saved on the work vehicle bought them otter food for a year and a large training pool on the ground floor. After a few more of these arguments, in which Gina demonstrated financial wisdom while remaining true to the project's vision, Solange put her in charge of the budget. She'd also turned over much of the PR tasks to Gina, including public speaking.

Solange's still-heavy French accent made it difficult for people to understand her. Her father had brought her to California when she was fifteen, and she remembered her teacher telling him that although she picked up her new language easily, she would probably never lose her accent, because she didn't learn

English before hitting puberty. Except for those few years when she lived in California with her father, Solange lived much of her life in Paris and, later, when she married Mustafa, Morocco.

Gina was not only easier to understand, but could answer any question about sea otters put to her.

"Don't sea otters compete with local fishermen? Isn't that why there's a ban on otters?" a man once asked.

"Otters do eat sea urchins, which on the surface of it makes them look like competitors with local fishermen, but they actually improve the health of the kelp beds, which are home to a huge variety of animals and fish. Left unchecked, sea urchins will eat an entire kelp forest to the seafloor, creating a marine desert. Everyone loses then," said Gina. "And to answer your second question, there was a ban at one time, created for several ill-advised reasons, but it's been lifted."

When the man asked why, Gina replied, "Well, for one thing, it wasn't very effective. You can't tell a sea otter where he can go. They're independent little cusses—and they don't read signs!"

Although not crazy about being in the spotlight, Gina had taken on these extra duties with a pragmatic shrug. So far, she had spoken at over a dozen fundraisers and the requisite environmental hearings. Whatever helped the otters.

Finally, avoiding the temptation to pass slow-moving traffic on the right, Gina made it to Main Beach. With directions from the shore patrol, within minutes she approached the spot where an athletic woman in khaki shorts was waving her down.

Grabbing her equipment from the jumble in the back seat, Gina slammed the gearshift into "Park," turned off the ignition, and jumped out of the car, making her way quickly across the warm sand to the woman who had flagged her down.

"Hi, I'm Logan, the one who called," she said, "and that's Amy, my daughter." Indicating the girl standing guard over the otters, she added, "She's the one who found them. Thanks for coming so quickly."

"Gina," she said, extending her free hand. "Gina Richards. Just glad I was there. I almost didn't come in today."

When they reached the otters, Gina knelt down to get a closer look. The girl created some shade by holding her Levi's jacket over the otters.

Gina did a preliminary assessment. The mother had been dead less than twenty-four hours. No colored tags on her rear flippers, eyes present, no foul odor or dark liquid oozing from the corpse, and flies but no maggots in the fur.

She didn't make these observations out loud.

Turning her attention to the otter she could save, the pup, who was breathing—just barely hanging on—Gina felt for broken bones and checked the pup's vitals.

"Should we keep it wet? We didn't know what to do . . . ," the girl asked, clearly upset, stepping back a little more so the vet could maneuver, but still hovering.

"You're doing fine . . ."

"Amy," the girl supplied. "And that's my mom, Logan." She mustn't have realized introductions had already been made. "We found them this morning. The tide was going out, and we almost lost them. We pulled them up, and . . . is the mother dead for sure?"

"You did the right thing, keeping the sun off her," Gina said, hoping to stem the girl's questions so she could concentrate.

"It's a her? You mean the baby or the mom?" Amy asked.

Focused entirely on the small life she was trying to save, the vet didn't respond.

It didn't look good. The tiny animal was too quiet. Most

otter pups were very vocal, emitting piercing sounds when they were anxious or hungry.

Probably in shock. She wouldn't know the extent of the pup's injuries until she got her cleaned up and on her table, but she came prepared. Transporting a newborn pup wasn't complicated. Making sure it survived the trip was the hard part.

Lifting her slowly off her mother's breast, she held her gently, checked her over, then administered a subcutaneous injection, giving the injured animal essential fluids and a hefty dose of antibiotics.

Finally, she remembered the two women were there. Logan and Amy had wisely stayed out of her way while she was working.

"Can one of you come along?" she asked. "My assistant's not in yet."

"I can!" Amy quickly volunteered, eagerly stepping forward.

"Good. There's a green carrier in the back of the Jeep—I need it—and there should be a towel. Bring them both over here so we can get this little girl to where I can hopefully help her."

Only one in ten orphaned pups was able to be saved, and even fewer qualified for rehabilitation. She would probably have to be euthanized, but Gina wasn't giving up yet.

Stay with me, little one.

Amy quickly complied, bringing the towel and carrier back to Gina, who instructed her to place the carrier on the sand and hold open the wire door.

Placing the pup gently inside, Gina latched it securely.

She turned to Logan. "Can you wait here for animal control?"

"Yes, of course," Logan said.

Once Amy was belted in the passenger side, Gina carefully put the carrier at her feet. It needed to be out of the wind and sun, and there was no time to snap on the Jeep's soft top. Gina did take the time to instruct Amy to don thick leather gloves. She was to steady the wire carrier but make sure her hands stayed on the outside.

"Even a baby sea otter can deliver a nasty bite," she warned, "especially an injured one."

"Shouldn't we wrap it in a blanket?"

"No, she'd overheat," Gina said.

She fired up the engine.

Hang in there, little girl.

"Shore patrol will be back with animal control soon. You can hitch a ride back with them."

5

Feeling useless, Logan watched as the Jeep sped away, skimming across the hard-packed sand, saltwater spraying out from under the tires.

Animal control got there quickly. Rolling the carcass unceremoniously onto a tarp and loading it in the back of their van only took a few minutes. They said they were taking it to the sea otter center.

The driver explained, "It's the law. Any sea otter found dead anywhere in California has to be examined to determine the cause of death."

"They do an autopsy on them?" Logan asked.

"It's called necropsy for animals," he said, showing off a little.

She had more questions, like why did they need to perform a necropsy when the cause of death was obvious—something had tried to take a bite out of this one—but she knew by the look on his face she'd exhausted the man's knowledge . . . and patience.

Besides, the flies had followed. It was time to go.

Opting to skip sharing the return trip with a dead sea mammal, Logan got a ride back with the lifeguards. On the way, she called Liam to let him know why they weren't back yet. He said he'd meet them at the center, but Logan told him she was already on her way to pick Amy up. Liam wouldn't hang up until she promised to bring Amy straight back to the cottage. Logan wasn't used to having to answer to anyone else in regards to her own daughter, but she reassured him she would.

Thirty minutes later, she was heading north on PCH, obeying most traffic laws. Making a left at Goldenrod, she drove past a larger-than-life, whiskered sea otter smiling down at her from a carved wooden sign.

Welcome to the Southern Sea Otter Sanctuary and Education Center

Quite a mouthful. They could call it SSOS for short, but saying the first two S's together made it sound like you had a speech impediment.

About one hundred feet in, the road came to a T. A small, clearly lettered sign directed school buses, delivery vehicles, and employees to the left, everyone else to the right. She went right and parked.

Crunching to a stop, she had her pick of spaces. She was relieved to see someone had left one of the large entrance doors propped open.

The artist's rendering on the brochure hadn't done it justice. The elegant building fit the landscape beautifully, perched on the edge of a bluff, overlooking a small cove bound by Devil's Claw on the south and a steep cliff on the right. Frank Lloyd Wright would have approved.

While the engine ticked, Logan got out of the car and regrouped. She had no idea what to expect when she went inside. If the pup didn't make it, she'd have to gather her heartbroken daughter back into the car and drive her home. She knew how attached Amy got to animals. When she was eight and her guinea pig died, she'd cried herself to sleep for a week.

The glass entrance doors were set in an undulating wall of colored tile. As she approached, the colors rolled through turquoise to bottle green to ultramarine blue, mimicking the constant movement of the Pacific. The effect was immediate. It felt as if she were swimming through a giant, playful wave.

Taking the open door as an invitation, she went in.

It took a minute for her eyes to adjust. Directly in front of her, a sleek reception desk sat in the middle of an airy space, curving to match the bend of the wall behind it.

Sea-star tiles embedded in the polished concrete floor created three meandering paths for visitors to follow: left, right, or straight past the desk to the back. To the right was the entrance to the gift shop. Long shades were drawn down inside all the floor-to-ceiling windows. Against vandals, she assumed. If it were already stocked, merchandise on open display would be quite a temptation.

About forty feet behind the counter, sunlight streamed in a couple of exit doors, beyond which she could see a short path. Framed by artistically arranged granite boulders and coastal scrub, the path went right up to the edge of the bluff, to a paved area with benches, a metal rail, and several telescopes facing toward the ocean. Breathtaking view.

A left turn at the reception desk took you toward what would be the main attraction: the otter exhibit. A velvet rope marked the entrance. Rescued animals who could not be released back into the wild successfully would serve as ambassadors to the public for their species.

Logan wondered if the pup would live long enough to be the first to enjoy the fancy new digs. She couldn't imagine how much something like this cost. All this for one group of animals, animals that, for most Southern Californians, were only a fond memory. Wanting to do more than help people *remember* sea otters, Solange wanted to bring them back, or at least support those who came back on their own. Logan read something to that effect in the SSOS mission statement on the back of the brochure. A lot of environmental groups were behind it: Friends of the Sea Otter, California Coastal Commission, StayWild, and others she hadn't heard of.

On the left, a low bench ran along the front wall, ending in a bank of elevators. Beyond that were several closed doors.

Not knowing which of those doors might lead to Amy, Logan had just about decided to try each one but was saved by the bell. Or the ding, anyway. One of the elevators opened, disgorging a smiling twentysomething man. He leaned out, blocking the doors to keep them from closing.

"Hi, you must be Logan. Come on back—everyone's downstairs."

His T-shirt boasted the same friendly otter face as the one that greeted her from the sign as she drove in.

"Thanks," she said, having to look slightly down to make eye contact. The man couldn't have been more than five foot six.

"Dennis," he said, offering his hand in a firm shake. "Gina's assistant."

6

There were three choices: "1," "2," and "L." He pushed the button for "2."

"How'd you know I was here?" Logan asked.

"Security cam. There's one hooked up in the lab, but it doesn't work yet. They started with the outside. We've had some vandalism. They're still adjusting it."

"Oh . . . how's the otter pup doing?"

"She's pretty weak, but if anyone can save her, Gina can. She was famous for taking on hopeless cases at the Slough."

"The Slough?"

"Yeah, Elkhorn Slough—it's an estuary about fourteen miles north of Monterey, one of the main field research areas. There are a bunch of sea otters up there. Well, not a bunch, but more than there are here. Gina was one of the vets in charge of the orphaned sea otter rehabilitation program at the aquarium."

Every time she heard the word, Logan told herself she was

going to find out exactly what *estuary* meant—some kind of water marsh, she thought. It seemed like a seventh grade science word she should know. She wanted to ask but waited a beat too long. The smooth elevator ride ended with a lurch.

"They need to fix that," Dennis said.

The high-end finishes of the public area upstairs did not extend to the first floor. This part of the center was obviously built for work, not show.

"It doesn't look like much, but it's got everything we need," Dennis said.

"Found her!" he announced. Looking like a cross between a science lab and an industrial kitchen, the twenty-by-thirty room was all white cabinets, buckets, and stainless steel sinks. Except for a set of sliding glass doors in the back, every inch of wall space was lined with pegboard, putting an impressive collection of knives, clamps, and hoses within easy reach. A large steel-topped island dominated the middle of the room.

That's where Amy was, sitting on a stool, watching Gina gently work on her little patient while Dennis picked up a clipboard to continue recording the results of the exam.

"One-point-eight kilograms."

Logan did the calculations in her head. About four pounds. That's not much less than Amy weighed. Born five weeks premature, she almost didn't make it. As soon as she came out, it was obvious something was wrong. All Logan saw before they whisked her baby away was the tiny infant's purple face. She'd been in labor so long she was too weak to lift her head. All she could do was lie there. No one told her what was going on.

She still remembered the rush of relief she felt when the nurse finally placed the living, breathing miracle in her arms. A halo of white-blond fuzz. Such soft, soft skin. And almost translucent, blue-veined eyelids. Perfect.

"It's a girl," the nurse had said, "and she's hungry."

Dennis's voice brought her back to the present.

"How's she doing?" he asked.

"She's QAR."

"Quiet, alert, and responsive," Dennis explained to Logan and Amy. He turned back to Gina. "Want me to fix up a bottle?"

"Yep, don't know how long it's been since this little girl ate. Blood sugar's low. We'll see if she accepts it."

After the pup had successfully sucked down her lunch, Gina carried her into an isolation room, placing her in a plain four-teen-by-six tank. A clear plexiglass wall gave Logan and Amy a good view.

Floating aimlessly like a furry cork, the pup opened her eyes. Two shiny black marbles set in a furry light-brown face looked all around, checking out her new world. Her fur looked lighter now that she was cleaned up. Paws, back flippers, and nose were black.

For a few seconds, Logan made eye contact with the pup. She swore it smiled, but it was probably only wiggling its whiskers. It looked so helpless, bobbing there, but also totally unconcerned, trusting that someone was going to take care of it. The resilience of life. Just a couple of hours ago, this newborn lay near death and almost certainly would be dead if Amy hadn't spotted her and help gotten there in time.

After a few minutes, Gina pulled the pup out onto a slightly raised platform lined with a rubber mat and began towel drying her. Another platform anchored the other end.

"That's the haul out," Dennis said. "Newborn pups can't do much more than float, so we have to do everything for them their mothers would do. You have to keep them clean and dry."

Amy, once again wearing her Levi's jacket, arms wrapped around herself to keep warm, kept her eyes glued on the pup as Gina completed the drying, then began combing and brushing its fur.

"If you don't keep their fur super clean, water gets in and they can get hypothermia and die," he said.

"Doesn't their blubber keep them warm?" Amy asked.

"Otters don't have a layer of blubber like seals do. They only have fur. Grooming like that traps air bubbles inside. Insulates them. It also stimulates their oil glands to keep the hair waterproof."

"Why does the tank have to be in a separate room?"

"It's an isolation tank—abandoned orphans don't have very strong immune systems."

"She wasn't abandoned. Her mother died," Amy said.

"Well, yeah, of course, she . . . that's just what they call any pup left on the beach . . . ," Dennis said. His voice trailed awkwardly.

Gina emerged from the small room, peeling off a pair of light-blue rubber gloves. Immediately, the newborn pup began to complain . . . *loudly.*

"Eeeeeee! Eeeeeee!"

"Make that VAR," Gina said with a wide smile. "*Vocal*, alert, and responsive."

Turning to Dennis, she added, "We'd better start a schedule."

Once a round-the-clock care and feeding schedule had been created, which Amy, of course, volunteered for, they rode the elevator back up to the main level. Amy said Liam would help, and Logan was pretty sure Brandon and Jeff would jump at the chance to help feed and care for a baby sea otter, too.

Logan suspected Liam would agree just to make sure Amy didn't tire herself out. Dennis took the night shift, with Gina on call. Amy, Liam, Logan, and her students, if they were available, were to arrive at 8:00 a.m. for training.

All the way on the elevator ride back up to the main floor, Amy continued peppering Dennis with questions. "When will she eat solid food? What do they eat?"

"Not yet, and she'll eat a lot of different foods eventually. Otters eat lobster, crab, clams, shrimp, oysters, octopus, abalone—all restaurant quality, too. They eat better than we do," he laughed, then added, "An adult sea otter has to eat about a third of its weight every day just to survive. The food bill for one otter can be over thirteen-thousand dollars a year."

That would probably be enough to keep a family of four in macaroni and cheese, Logan thought.

They said goodbye at the door, which Dennis closed behind them, promising to be on time in the morning.

Not only was Logan almost as excited as Amy about being able to work up close and personal with a baby sea otter, she also wanted to make sure her daughter didn't overdo it. With all of them sharing responsibility for just one shift during the day, if Amy needed a break, they could make sure she got one. Gina said she was welcome to the cot in her office any time.

On the drive back toward the cottage, the adrenaline that had carried Amy through the otter pup's rescue was obviously depleted. Before they pulled onto PCH, Logan looked over at her. Head resting against the window, she was already half asleep.

7

Exhaustion didn't hit Gina until the sun was well over the yardarm. Sinking into her chair, elbows on her desk, she rubbed the back of her neck. Dennis should be here soon. She sent him home earlier, for a few hours' rest before starting his shift. She had an apartment in town but planned on staying here tonight. She didn't want to be too far away. At least the first few nights.

Otter 1 was doing fine, but the chances for any orphaned pup were extremely low. Not only did they have to survive the first few weeks, but then they had to learn how to be otters. Gina knew their job would be to teach Otter 1 to swim, dive, find food, groom herself, avoid danger, and do all the other things necessary for her successful survival in her natural habitat. Only about ten percent of rescued otter pups achieved the skills and health necessary to be released back into the wild and live long enough to mate and have pups of their own. And that was the gold standard—to increase the southern sea otter population in the wild.

To keep this goal in mind and avoid getting too attached, rescued pups were given a number, not a name.

Until an hour ago, Gina hadn't decided whether or not to dedicate the hours and resources necessary to rehabilitate the pup. Of course, that's what she wanted to do for every otter—that's one reason Solange had built this place—but it wasn't always possible. With a tremor of excitement and hope, she contemplated the work ahead.

Tomorrow, she'd break out the Darth Vader suits. Her volunteers wouldn't like them, but they were necessary. Consisting of a black welder's mask and a big, dark rain poncho, the suit broke up a handler's visual human form and kept the otters from becoming tame.

The next few days would be busy, but she'd have to fit in the necropsy on the mother. These necropsies provided valuable data for understanding the subtle and sometimes layered causes of death, as well as general data on the recovering population. Although there were about twenty-seven hundred individual southern sea otters at last count, recovery was stalled. No one really knew why.

Gina also knew she should make a phone call. She was technically breaking the law. According to US Fish and Wildlife, every injured or abandoned sea otter was to be taken to Monterey Bay Aquarium, the only center authorized to care for them. As a former Monterey Bay Aquarium employee, she had explained this patiently to many a well-meaning citizen who rescued an otter, thinking they could keep them in a tub of sea water in their garage. Luckily, the animal control officers hadn't questioned her authority.

Gina found herself in the awkward position of being on the other end this time. Now that she no longer worked for the aquarium, *she* was the unauthorized person wanting to take care of an orphaned otter pup. She was more than capable, and although the Southern Sea Otter Sanctuary was state-of-the-art, it was not yet officially recognized. Of course, her facility and her expertise were a far cry from someone's garage. They were created specifically to handle this kind of situation, but still. Eventually, she'd have to make that call.

She leaned back in her squeaky chair. Better to ask for forgiveness than permission.

"In for a penny, in for a pound," Gina said out loud.

"No pennies necessary," Dennis said, dropping a bright, white In-N-Out bag on her desk. "Double-Double. Large fries, crispy. Sauce on the side. Diet Coke."

He sat down opposite her and took out his own burger and drink. His was a lemonade. In-N-Out made the best.

Until the smell of greasy French fries hit her, Gina hadn't realized how hungry she was.

"You are a god!"

As they ate dinner, she brought him up to date on Otter 1's progress so far, pushing aside her notes for tomorrow's necropsy of the mother. Animal control brought her in this morning, and she was in the cooler in the lab.

Dennis, leaving Gina to her paperwork, mixed up another gourmet clam shake for the pup and entered the isolation room.

"Eeeeeee! Eeeeeee! Eeeeeee!"

It was going to be a long night.

8

MONDAY, JULY 6, 2015

Logan pulled a long, luxurious breath of salt air into her lungs and looked out over the rocky cove below. Hearing the ocean from her rooftop deck was one thing, but standing on the observation deck of the sea otter center, directly over the crashing waves, left her awestruck. Nature was amazing. It would surely cure any part of you that was broken.

Just a few more minutes. Pushing back from the railing, she stretched her back flat and away, into a modified version of downward-facing dog. Mid stretch she got a good pop.

Man, that felt good.

June gloom was history, and after the morning marine layer burned off, July days were bright and warm. Every summer had its rhythm, and this year's was turning into just the right mix of work and play. Amy was home and healing. Liam seemed good for her. She and Ben felt right. Fractals was running smoothly—they'd be ready for the new school year. The new recordings with Jeff and Brandon were even better than the last ones. Everything was better than she could have hoped.

That should have been her clue.

Since Thursday, when they discovered the abandoned otter pup, she and Amy had been coming out to the sea otter center every morning for otter duty. Amy was a natural.

Liam joined them at the center the first few days, but soon realized three people on one shift was overkill. He'd been making himself more useful working on the kelp-bed restoration project with one of the local conservation groups they'd met at Tava'e's.

A visiting cousin of Tava'e's, a man in his forties named Amosa, who worked with one of them, offered to take Liam out to see the section they were working on now.

"We can always use another hand, bro," he'd said.

When Liam told him he couldn't swim, Amosa was surprised, but undaunted. He promptly included swimming, paddling, and snorkeling lessons in his offer. In the meantime, they used a boat.

Both men grew up on islands, surrounded by miles of ocean, but the ocean surrounding Liam's island had a mean temperature of forty-nine degrees Fahrenheit. Not exactly swimmer friendly.

As Logan predicted, Jeff and Brandon enthusiastically signed on for the opportunity to work with a baby sea otter. Both boys managed to rearrange their summer job schedules to mornings. Gina put them on an afternoon shift that didn't start until 2:00 p.m., so it worked out. Jeff always got there early so he could see Amy. Logan didn't want to butt in, but her daughter seemed to be completely oblivious to Jeff's crush on her. If she didn't sit her down soon and talk about ways to let the boy down gently, they'd have one heartbroken kid on their hands.

"Mom!" Amy called from inside.

Reluctantly, Logan left her ocean view for the darkened lab. It took her eyes a minute to adjust.

"Gina said she'd be right back. Dennis's truck broke down. She's going out to pick him up. She said we could get started without her."

Amy was already heading for the isolation-tank room.

Logan's phone chose that moment to ring.

"Okay, hon, go ahead and get started. I'll be right there," Logan said, heading back out onto the deck for better reception.

If Logan had looked back, she would have seen Amy grab her black poncho and mask from the hook on the wall, go inside, but not put them on. She also would have seen her scoop the tiny creature up into her arms after she hauled out and nuzzle against her fur as she towel dried her, whispering, "Sadie! How's my girl?" going against all of Gina's clearly laid out rules.

"Hello, Charles," Logan answered the phone, wondering why Charles Greuger was calling. He was the school board member responsible for hiring her to run the music/math program they'd named Fractals, but she hadn't had much contact with him directly since the program got off the ground. He told her his philosophy was to hire good people, then let them do their jobs. Once he put her in touch with Mrs. Houser, the woman whose generous donations got the program off the ground initially and kept it going, he'd gone back to doing whatever it is superintendents do.

Logan was grateful. Their arrangement wouldn't have lasted long if he'd been a micromanager.

"Good morning, Logan. Did I catch you in the middle of something, or are you free to talk?" he said.

"No, I can talk—I'm down here at the sea otter center, so

it's a little noisy out here, but I lose the connection inside. Can you hear me over the seagulls?"

"Yes, yes, I can hear you just fine," he said.

"What can I do for you?" Logan asked.

"Well, I'm afraid I have some sad news, Logan. Mrs. Houser has died," he said.

The man didn't pull any punches.

"Oh my God, when? I didn't even know she was sick. I mean, we just talked last week, and she sounded fine!"

"It was sudden. She had a stroke. Her family didn't give me any more details than that," he said.

"Oh, well of course," Logan said. "Is there anything we can do? When you find out if a memorial service or funeral will be held, I'd like to—I'm sure everyone from Fractals will want to be there. I . . . She seemed so healthy. I'm just so surprised."

"Yes, we're all in a bit of shock here, too." He paused, then continued, "I'll let you know as soon as I do about the service. And Logan . . . let's get together next week. I'm sure it's nothing to worry about, but Mrs. Hauser hadn't yet deposited the funds to the district for your program for the upcoming school year."

All funds, large or small, that financed Fractals or any other district-run program went through district special accounts. From there, employees were paid directly by the district as TOSAs, teachers on special assignment, so they wouldn't lose their years of service. Another check was issued to the Fractals' account that Logan administered.

"I was going to give her a call, but of course now, I don't want to bother the family at a time like this."

"Oh, of course. I agree," Logan said.

"Okay then—I'll have my secretary give you a call in a day or two to set something up for next week if you're available.

I'm sure by then the deposit will have been made. Mrs. Houser gave to many charitable foundations. She must have established contingencies for something like this."

Logan assured him she would make herself available and asked him to convey her condolences to the family. She would miss the sharp septuagenarian, but the practical side of her couldn't help worrying about the funding.

Mrs. Houser was Fractals' major financial supporter. Without her last two major donations, the program would come to a screeching halt, and they were just getting started. She was so impressed with the positive effect the program had on children, she'd said she was taking steps to make her annual donations permanent.

Logan was so grateful the woman saw beyond state tests. No test measured enthusiasm or love of learning, let alone the synergistic nature of music and math in the human brain.

If the money didn't show up in the next couple of weeks, Logan knew everyone who worked so hard in the program would be affected. They'd be scrambling for positions when most had already been filled for the new school year. Being permanent employees with the district, they had some rights and would still have jobs, just not the ones they'd given up. The district could place them at any school, any subject, any grade level.

Bonnie once told Logan about a teacher made to teach middle school PE when she'd spent the last twenty-six years teaching kindergarten. This was a tried-and-true method the district used to force teachers who rocked the boat to retire.

Being highly qualified teachers, Tilly and Jeremy would probably find work, but Logan, only having taught in the classroom as a substitute teacher for a year, had no such security. If Fractals was dismantled due to lack of funding, she would be out of a job. Again.

9

"**Y**ou need a break."

Logan looked up from the clutter of paper she'd accumulated on the kitchen counter. Ben's frame filled the doorway. He came in and kissed her on the forehead.

What time was it anyway?

She'd been making calls and trying to put out fires since after lunch.

"You're right," she said. "I'm just spinning my wheels here anyway."

"Good!" Ben said, sounding pleased.

"Grab your beach stuff. Amy and Liam are going to meet us down at Pirate's Cove. I've got supplies—we're doing an early picnic dinner."

Logan's eyes lit up. Amy had been feeling so much better. After making sure her phone was on and charged, she forced herself to leave it on the kitchen counter. Since they were going to be with Amy, there was no reason to take it. All other calls could wait.

In Southern California, wardrobe changes are easy. Already wearing a T-shirt and shorts, Logan grabbed a hooded sweatshirt, some flip-flops, and a baseball hat. Mr. Prepared always kept sunscreen in his car.

On the drive down, Logan told him about the private tour of SSOS and up-close-and-personal visit with a certain baby sea otter she'd arranged with Gina for the boys. Dennis would do the actual tour, but Logan knew enough to ask the woman in charge for permission before asking him.

"They'll love that." Ben reached over and squeezed her leg.

Pirate's Cove was only four miles south of Main Beach, but with tourist traffic, it took forty minutes to reach. It was worth the drive, though. Known mostly only to locals, it was off a small side street. You parked, walked a couple of blocks, looked for the tall red house, and turned right. After a sharp left turn, you found the winding, unmarked, hidden set of stairs to the beach, put in years ago by the residents on either side. As long as you respected their space, they were okay with you using the path.

This afternoon, it was glorious. Shielded by the rocks on either side, Pirate's Cove was not only devoid of tourists, but absolutely sparkled. Picture postcard perfect.

Amy and Liam were already there, blanket spread and waiting.

Ben set the picnic basket down, shook hands with Liam, and gave Amy a hug. Liam had a nervous smile and an ice-filled bucket dug into the sand next to him. Eyes sparkling mischievously, Amy was kneeling, sitting up on her heels on the blanket next to Liam.

Something was obviously up.

Before Logan could ask what was going on, Amy popped up off the blanket and wiggled the fingers of her left hand, showing off a single brilliant emerald, flanked by diamonds, on a smooth platinum band. It was stunning. Logan couldn't help but wonder how Liam could afford such a ring.

"We're engaged!" Amy said.

"I hope it's all right, Mrs. McKenna," Liam said. "I know Amy already said yes in Africa, but I wanted to make it official and ask you in person if it is okay if I marry your daughter."

It took half a beat for everything to register, during which Liam looked stricken, but Logan recovered quickly and reassured Liam he was welcome in the family.

She looked directly into the young man's eyes and added, "I couldn't have chosen anyone better for Amy. You two are a perfect match."

Tears flowed and more hugs were given and received. Liam pulled out the bottle of champagne, fumbled with it, and finally gave it to Ben, who opened it deftly and filled the plastic champagne flutes he'd spirited out of his picnic basket.

The sun set right on cue.

Life does have its moments.

10

"What time are Bonnie and Mike coming?" Ben asked, checking the temperature on the grill.

"Around six. Just Bonnie, though. Mike's working tonight," Logan said, counting chairs.

Mike was a firefighter, and Bonnie credited his twenty-four-on, forty-eight-off schedule for keeping their marriage intact.

"Are the boys coming?"

"Not sure. I think they're at camp still, but if they do come, Cooper and Calvin will have someone to play with." Calvin and Cooper were Ben's nephews. Cooper's first name was Trent, but last year, when a girl in his class told him she liked his middle name because it was cool, he'd refused to go by anything else, so Cooper it was.

Their mom, Ben's sister, was away on bridesmaid duty for one of her sorority sisters.

Since the wedding was within spitting distance of Pebble Beach, his brother-in-law went along to play golf. The boys were staying with their uncle for the weekend.

Ages eleven and twelve, both boys were becoming accomplished surfers. They spent the whole day at the beach and were back down there now, giving Purgatory a run. They'd be back by dinner, though. Their BBQ radar was well tuned. As was Purgatory's. If for any reason they forgot, the dog would drag them home in time.

"Thomas and Lisa?" he called back over his shoulder.

"Definitely. They didn't get to see Amy last time, remember? They were out in Colorado still. They haven't met Liam yet."

Ben went back into the house to pull some more burgers out of the freezer.

Logan did a last-minute count to make sure she had a place for everyone.

Bonnie, me and Ben, Amy and Liam, the boys, Rick and Paula, Thomas and Lisa . . .

Yes, she was good. The picnic table seated twelve.

Damn! She forgot Ned and Sally and their precocious toddler.

No worries—they'd just pull up a couple more chairs. She started scooching some of the place settings over to make room.

Logan and Ben usually BBQ'd at her place Sunday nights, then finished the evening on the rooftop deck, snuggling under a blanket. But tonight's dinner had turned into something of a welcome-home/engagement party, so they decided to set up at Ben's. He had more room. Her side yard and his backyard blended into each other anyway, so there was plenty of room for kids and dogs to play.

Putting his landscape-architect skills to good use, Ben's back patio was not only functional, but attractive. Last summer, he and some friends added an attractive L-shaped outdoor kitchen, complete with built-in chopping blocks, large double sink, plenty of storage under the black granite counter, and, Ben's pride and joy, a generously proportioned gas grill. There was even a small under-the-counter refrigerator. This he kept supplied with five different kinds of mustard, hot sauces, gourmet olives, his favorite IPA, and a selection of nonalcoholic beverages for the kids. Tonight, he'd added a bowl of his famous garlic aioli. He planned on serving that with the steamed artichokes.

A rice cooker quietly hissed on the counter to the left of the grill. Logan checked the time. Five more minutes. Going back to the house, she grabbed a broad wooden spoon and a stack of deep bowls.

"I don't think there's room for this on the table. How 'bout if we just have everyone fill their bowls up from here?"

"Good idea," Ben said. "There's butter in there, too, if you want to put some out along with the soy sauce."

Johnny Cash at full volume let them know Rick and Paula had arrived. Logan looked up from dragging another chair over to the picnic table.

She raised her eyebrows at Ben. Charlie usually sat in front, but she'd been relegated to the back seat since Paula moved in. The dog didn't seem to mind, though. On a signal from Rick, Charlie launched herself out of the car and bounded around the corner of the house, looking for Purgatory.

Off duty, Charlie was in play mode.

The guests of honor arrived next. Amy still looked thin, but not as pale as a few days ago. A week of sea otter duty, and getting engaged, obviously suited her. With the help of a curling iron, she'd arranged her normally stick-straight hair into long, loose waves, curling around the straps of a blue-and-yellow flowered sundress. With Amy tucked under Liam's protective arm, they both glowed.

"I made her take a nap before we came," Liam said to Logan. Comfortably and conservatively dressed in khakis and a polo shirt, he released Amy only to shake hands as introductions were made.

After first asking what the doctor would allow in the way of alcoholic beverages, Ben got Amy a tall iced tea. The tropical disease specialist said she was doing well. As long as she didn't overexert herself and avoided the heat of the day or getting chilled, he wouldn't need to see her for another two weeks. Liam took her vitals morning and night and kept a record of her food intake and sleep.

Ben walked Liam over to the grill and showed him where the beer was. He grabbed a Sierra Nevada.

"I'll take one of those," Ben said.

The two men talked comfortably, periodically checking on the meat thermometer stuck in the tri-tip at the back of the grill. Ben was waiting to add the burgers and dogs until everyone arrived. A huge pot of salted water simmered on one of the two burners to the left. Ben turned up the gas, brought it to a boil, then lowered a large metal basket of cleaned and trimmed artichokes into the water.

Ned and Sally got there just as Ben and Liam were taking the meat off the grill. Thomas and Lisa apologized for being late. He still did occasional flint-knapping demos at the Otter Festival.

Bonnie, the last to arrive, came sailing in, still talking on the phone. With a dramatic huff, she firmly turned off her phone. Holding it with two fingers, as if it might bite her at any minute, she dropped it into her purse.

Ben raised his eyebrows.

"I'm afraid to ask how *your* day went," Logan said.

Bonnie was having trouble with one of her kids, a volatile teen named Haley. Last week they caught her trying to sneak out of the house, wearing a too-tight top and spray-on shorts. An older-model Mustang screeched away from the curb just as Mike flipped on the lights, catching her in the act. The getaway car belonged to a sixteen-year-old loser named Brent. Since this was a repeat offense, she'd been grounded, her fifteenth birthday party canceled. Ever since, she'd been giving her parents the silent treatment.

If Haley thought she'd wear them down, she was wrong.

Mike recruited their neighbor, a retired cop, to keep an eye on her whenever one of them couldn't be there. She also had to be ready to FaceTime her parents whenever either of them called to check in.

Modern technology had its advantages.

"How was my day?" Bonnie repeated. "Well, no one's in jail or in the hospital. That counts as a *great* day! Where are you hiding the beer, Ben? I soooo need one!"

11

Nothing kept Bonnie down for long. Within minutes she was deep in conversation talking interior design with Paula, who wanted to give Rick's bachelor pad a makeover and couldn't have found a more perfect coconspirator. Bonnie lived to decorate. What she didn't know about fabric, furniture, and paint hadn't been invented yet.

With everything on the table, it was time to eat. Both dogs parked themselves at the boys' feet, knowing they were the softest touches when it came to sneaking food under the table. For the next thirty minutes, everyone ate, talked, and reached for seconds.

Bonnie's potato salad was a hit, as was Lisa's stack of fry bread, kept warm in a thick cotton towel.

"Where have you been all my life?" Ben moaned, helping himself to another piece. Smothering it with a scoop of Mike's firehouse chili, which Bonnie brought per his request, he folded it over and took a huge bite.

"They're good for dessert, too, Ben," Lisa tempted. "A little powdered sugar and honey. Mmmm . . ."

"Oh yeah!" Bonnie chimed in.

By nine, everyone, including the humans, was stuffed. Looking across the table at Ben, who was listening as Amy repeated the story of the rescued otter pup for Lisa and Thomas, Logan felt a swell of love. Not one to cry, she felt herself tearing up.

Must be the wine.

It *had* been a long day. Hell, it had been a long week. A long three years. Logan cleared her throat and blinked before she gave in to sentiment completely.

Ben's nephews asked to be excused as soon as they'd inhaled their food. They wanted to play Frisbee with the dogs on the small patch of lawn Ben kept clear for them. Knowing Purgatory's potentially lethal, gassy response to Polish sausages, of which he'd eaten no less than four, all of the adults readily agreed.

As the evening wound down, Ben's nephews went inside to play video games, and strings of solar-powered garden lights twinkled on overhead. Crisscrossed above the patio from the grill to the back door, they softly lit the scene. Perfect.

Everyone she loved was sitting around this table. Amy was home safe. Getting stronger every day, thanks in large part to Liam. Thomas and Lisa never looked happier. Ben, of course. He'd become a beautiful part of her life. Bonnie. She would work it out with her daughter. She and Mike were great parents.

Around ten, Liam started making time-to-leave noises, but Amy begged for some music.

"Just a few more minutes? I haven't heard them play in ages. I promise to go straight to bed when we get home," she said.

Sally shifted Quin, who'd fallen asleep on her mother's lap, into Lisa's arms and went inside to get their instruments. Ned had stashed them next to the couch in the den with some toys they'd brought for Quin.

Logan crossed the backyard to her place to get her violin. Excited about playing, she almost tripped on a paving stone. Between her place and Ben's, there was adequate light, but only if she paid attention.

Safely across both yards, she sat down on one of the chairs Ben had set up. She lifted Bella out of her case and tuned up with Ned and Sally for their impromptu concert.

"We don't take requests, only tips!" Ned informed his audience a little too loudly.

They all knew this was not true, as Ned knew every song ever written and loved the challenge. And if he didn't know a song, he'd make one up.

Logan hoped the neighbors liked bluegrass.

They wowed the crowd with rousing renditions of "Foggy Mountain Breakdown" and "Cumberland Gap," which showcased Ned's banjo skills, before settling into his signature song, "Salty Dog Blues," which he always sang directly to Sally. Knowing the song was coming, Ben brought out a round of real salty dogs: salt-rimmed glasses with a simple blend of fresh-squeezed grapefruit juice and Ketel One. Ben made his with gin but bowed to modern tastes for the vodka version.

They slowed things down some for the next few songs. Sally's buttery alto sounded for all the world just like Alison Krauss. When they got to "If I Didn't Know Any Better," Logan wished she could sing a love song like that to Ben. The best she could do was close her eyes and pour her soul into playing Bella, hoping the music carried her message to the man she was falling deeper in love with every day.

Halfway through "Whiskey Lullaby," an ambulance, red and blue lights flashing and siren blaring, barreled north on PCH, tearing through the light at the base of Killer Hill.

Several patrol cars followed.

Paula pulled out her phone. A dispatcher with the Jasper Police Department, she knew just whom to call.

Rick checked his pager, ready to roll if he was called in. Charlie's ears pricked up, and she trotted over to sit next to Rick, ramrod straight.

All eyes were on Paula.

"Possible explosion and injury on Goldenrod and PCH," relayed Paula to the group.

Turning to Logan, Ned asked, "Isn't that . . . ?"

"That's the sea otter center!" said Amy.

Logan resisted the urge to jump into her car and go find out what was happening. She wanted to go help, but common sense told her she would only be in the way right now.

Amy also started for the car, but Rick caught her arm and convinced his niece to stay put. He ticked off the reasons.

"You won't be able to get anywhere near that center. Not until the injured have been cared for, the scene secured, and the techs complete their work. *Definitely* not tonight."

Amy stood there glaring at him, arms stubbornly folded.

"You are *just* like your mother," Rick said, holding his ground.

Knowing there was nothing anyone could do right now, Logan funneled her energy into things over which she did have control: packing up instruments, clearing the table, putting leftovers in the refrigerator. Amy let Liam take her home, but only after repeated promises from her uncle and mother that someone would call her as soon as they knew anything.

Everyone gathered their things and said their goodbyes. Rick promised to call Logan in the morning and let her know what was happening. The best thing any of them could do was to stay home and get some rest.

Back in her kitchen later that night, Logan looked at the calendar taped on the refrigerator. They were supposed to do their volunteer shifts in the morning. She'd have to call first to see if Gina still wanted them to come in.

She hated not knowing what was going on—whether Gina and Dennis were okay. And Otter 1. That little animal was definitely having a run of bad luck.

Maybe the dispatcher made a mistake and no one had been injured.

12

Dazed, Gina sat on the edge of the fountain in front, wrapped in a silver shock blanket, and stared at what used to be the entrance to the center.

Two EMTs, gingerly stepping over broken glass, carried someone on a litter out of a gaping hole. With speed and efficiency, they loaded him into the back of an ambulance.

A young patrol officer named Drummond walked over. Introducing himself, he began taking down an incident report. He jotted her answers into a small lined notebook, which surprised her. She assumed they only had those in the movies—that they'd have some high-tech replacement by now.

Gina did her best to answer.

"Yes, he works here. His name is Dennis—Dennis Radmore."

"Twenty-six—no, maybe twenty-seven. He's my assistant. I'll have to check his exact age. I have his records inside, in my office."

"No. No family. Well, he has a sister in Idaho, but I don't

know her name, or where she is or how to locate her. They're estranged. Both parents are deceased."

She felt like she was beginning to babble. Maybe she was.

Officer Drummond excused himself for a minute to give this information to the ambulance driver as she hopped in the front seat and buckled in. Her partner nodded that he got it. Within seconds, the emergency vehicle went wailing toward PCH, kicking up gravel and dust. Lights flashing, it turned north.

"Where are they taking him?"

"Hoag Hospital. They have a surgeon waiting. They said you did an excellent job of first aid. It's because of you he's alive."

Gina nodded. She was a vet. If she couldn't apply pressure to a wound and dial 911, she should turn in her license.

"Now, Ms. Richards, I need to ask you a few more questions. I need you to start at the beginning. Tell me everything you can remember. Where were you? Did you hear anything?"

Ignoring his question, Gina asked one of her own, "When can I go to the hospital? He's just a kid. He'll need someone there when he wakes up."

"I understand your concern, but this won't take long."

Gina's mind cleared a bit. Officer Drummond probably didn't think anyone aged twenty-seven qualified as being a kid—he couldn't be older than twenty-nine himself—but to each his own.

"Okay," she said, refocusing, "but I'm doing this inside. I've got an orphaned sea otter in there, a wild animal, and she can't be left alone this long."

"I'm sorry, but we can't let you in the building until the crime-scene team completes their—"

"Well, they'll just have to work around me," Gina said, standing up, her natural personality asserting itself. "My office is on the second level where the otter tank is, and nothing happened on that level. We can talk there."

Officer Drummond agreed to conduct the interview in her office, as long as they used the employee entrance on the left side of the building, away from the break-in. Still, he gave her some booties before they went in, just in case, saying you never knew how far the crime scene reached.

As they walked past the front of the building and around to the side, Gina saw the damage up close. Both large entry doors, and a good part of the window wall on each side, had been completely blown out, as if the building had been peeled back by a giant can opener. She could see through to where she'd discovered Dennis. When she'd rushed up from the lab, looking for him, he'd been out cold on the floor just past the elevator, lying facedown on the polished concrete, not moving. Blood still pooled on the floor.

She looked away.

That's when she ran back down to get her bag and called 911.

Although it went against her grain, for the next twenty minutes, Gina focused on the officer's questions. Maybe if she answered them thoroughly enough now, they'd leave sooner.

After Officer Drummond cleared the lab and both offices, Gina checked on the pup, donning the poncho and mask. Otter 1 was fine, although indignant at being left alone for so long. Gina fixed her a shake, let her swim some, then pulled up another chair for the officer while she hauled out the pup and began to vigorously towel dry her fur. She should have made him wear the Darth Vader suit, too, but she doubted Otter 1 would ever see him again, and he wasn't going to interact with the animal.

Grooming Otter 1 calmed Gina as well as the young animal. She managed to tell the officer what little she knew.

Her "otter mom" shift had ended at 8:00 p.m., when Dennis took over. She had set her alarm for 4:00 a.m. She planned on sleeping at the center for the next few days, until Otter 1 was settled in. There was a cot in her office.

Exhausted from the intensive rescue efforts of the last twenty-four-hours, she was out like a light the minute her head hit the pillow. At some point after that—she wasn't sure of the exact time—something jolted her out of a deep sleep.

While her disoriented brain tried to make some sense of what woke her—probably just a small earthquake, they'd had several recently—she went to see if Otter 1 was all right.

Otter 1 was okay, but Dennis wasn't with her, so Gina took the emergency stairs up to the main floor to find him. She thought the elevator might be jammed if it was an earthquake that had awakened her. She was halfway up the stairs when she felt and heard the second explosion.

"Did you see anyone? Was anyone running away?"

"No, I didn't see anyone."

"What about a vehicle? Did you see any cars in the parking lot?"

"No, I'm sorry. It was dark. I went immediately to help Dennis. I didn't see anyone."

"As far as you can tell, has anything been disturbed or taken down here?"

"No, everything looks the same here. Like I said, I didn't see or hear anything on this floor."

"Has anything like this ever happened before?"

"We had some vandalism," Gina admitted, "graffiti on the outside of the building, broken beer bottles . . . trash. Probably just local kids blowing off steam, but nothing like this."

"What about security cameras?"

"Yes, Solange was in the process of installing them. The

exterior ones should be working. I'll show you the video."

The video files turned out to be of only marginal help. They did record two men, dressed in jeans, work shoes, and baggy hooded sweatshirts, but showed only a shadow of their faces. One had a backpack. They approached the building from the parking lot, silhouetted by the lights mounted on the pole. The cameras were not angled properly near the doors, so they did not pick up the actual placement of the explosives or give any clues as to what type were used. And the men had either walked in or parked out of camera range.

Clearly disappointed the video didn't provide better information, Officer Drummond said, "Could be anybody—they look like any construction worker you'd see around here."

Still, he said he'd make sure it all got included in the report and put in the file.

He asked a few more questions and took Gina's contact number and address. Said he'd be in touch tomorrow to give her a case number for their insurance.

Ugh. Insurance.

Filling out insurance claims ranked way down on her personal totem pole of priorities, after Dennis and Otter 1, but she'd do it. It was her job.

After the crime-scene techs did a sweep of the area, Gina obtained permission to remain at the center that night, as long as she limited her access to the lab and tank areas. Once she explained Otter 1's schedule couldn't be altered, they gave permission for the volunteers she had just trained to cover their shifts the next day, as long as they, too, remained on level two with her. Officer Drummond got their names, said they'd all have to be interviewed.

Gina was fine with being limited to this floor tonight. She had no desire to go upstairs. Plenty of time for her to deal with that tomorrow. She was no stranger to blood, but she'd never had to clean up a friend's.

When the officer left, Gina called Solange to fill her in. The police had already contacted her, but she appreciated hearing from Gina. Said she'd be down in the morning and for Gina to get some rest. Police said they'd keep a car there overnight.

Next, Gina contacted Logan McKenna. Apologizing for calling so late, she explained the situation.

Something about the McKenna woman inspired confidence. Gina asked her to contact the other volunteers and get them to the center tomorrow. They could figure out a new schedule then. Logan said she could be there early. Gina would just have to wait until then to go to the hospital. Already 3:00 a.m. Only a few more hours.

Fires put out for now, her mind turned to Dennis. It was her fault. She brought him down here. He'd been one of the best Monterey Bay Aquarium volunteers at the Slough. He didn't have any family to speak of, so he jumped at the chance to have an actual, full-time, paying job working with otters.

"Eeeeeee!"

In spite of herself, Gina smiled wearily.

Otter 1 was calling.

Nature had a way of pushing all human concerns aside.

13

Solange disconnected the call and took a long pull on her cigarette, releasing the smoke slowly through deeply lined lips. This must be related.

A lifelong insomniac, she was awake when Gina called. She liked it up here in her father's studio, sitting in the dark. She still thought of it as his, even though he gave it to her when he died.

Everything was hers. This house, all his art, and several pieces of property. She'd never paid attention to them. She let her accountant keep up with the taxes, make sure someone cleared the brush—whatever it was one did to maintain property. Between the still-successful sales of her own work; a small sum her late husband, Mustafa, left her; and the rest of her inheritance, she could afford to ignore those pieces of land. Until now.

The first letter came in January. When the letters kept coming, she hired an attorney. She thought the whole issue would be resolved by now, but it was already July.

She'd have to tell Gina soon. So many people had put in long hours and donated talent, time, and money to make the Southern Sea Otter Sanctuary a reality. If this violence was related, they deserved to be notified.

She looked toward the large picture windows that took up the wall facing the ocean, and her reflection stared back at her. Short, thinning white hair. Pieces pulled forward. Delicately arched eyebrows framed dark-grey eyes. Chic was a word often used to describe Solange.

She stood and walked to the windows. No more than five five in heels, which she never wore. During her student days, she most often tucked herself into sturdy men's overalls and work boots. Sculpting was not a dainty art.

Then there was her Moroccan period. Lots of skirts, scarves, and color. The years with Mustafa were good ones. They worked. They loved. And then he got sick. She lost him just before news of her father's death that same year. When she returned to California, she settled into her work. It cleared her mind. Fewer choices to make.

Suddenly needing oxygen, she pushed the center window open a little farther. Cold sea air moistened and refreshed her eyes. The sound of ocean waves drifted in. Both hands on the windowsill, she leaned out in order to breathe it all in. She loved this view. Organically extended from a granite outcrop at the top of a narrow canyon, her father built a home any modern architect would have loved.

Far below, the Pacific Ocean rippled away to the horizon to meet a navy sky. Shreds of clouds obscured the stars. Moonlight made abstract splotches of a jumble of rooftops collected at the bottom of the canyon. Just beyond the rooftops, a thick black line, broken now and then by clumps of coastal oak, cottonwood, and pine, separated the homes from the beach. A long ribbon of silver sand stretched south, dissolving into the dark.

The north end of the beach, a couple of miles away, ended abruptly at the stark black cutout of Devil's Claw. Blue-white scalloped lace edged the waves slipping up onto the shore.

She heard no otters but knew there was at least one nearby.

And there could be more. There was no reason why this area could not be restored. Now that the law had changed and sea otters were once again allowed to range freely, more and more of them would make it down this far.

After a few more minutes, Solange returned to the drafting table and pulled out the small drawer on the side. In it was the copy of the letter, and several more official items of correspondence regarding her property at Goldenrod and Pacific Coast Highway, otherwise known as lot 429.

She'd been dealing with this for months now, ever since the attorney Mr. Schofield had contacted her. Or his office had. She was sure the letters she'd received were boilerplate ones, full of capital letters and legalese—meant to intimidate. Still, the man was insistent. His client wasn't giving up.

Well, neither was she.

His client. Someone named Scott, claiming to be her half brother.

They'd even sent her attorney a copy of the letter. Obviously fake.

But maybe he was tired of waiting and was upping the intimidation from simple vandalism to attacking employees at the center. Solange didn't know if any of the recent attacks on the center were related to the title dispute, but she couldn't have people's lives in danger.

She'd have to find a way to settle this once and for all but had no idea how. The thought that someone would stoop so low—not just destroying property, but putting people's lives in danger. It was beyond her.

If it was just money, she'd give it to him gladly. Money had never meant that much to her.

But the Southern Sea Otter Sanctuary and Education Center wasn't about making money. It was unique and vitally important to the restoration of not only this one marine mammal, but the whole Southern California coastline.

She couldn't imagine losing it. Even if she had the money to buy another piece of property, there was no other coastal property as uniquely situated as this one. Even if they could find another land donor, there simply wasn't another location as perfect as lot 429, and she didn't know if she could raise the money to rebuild the center somewhere else.

From what her attorney had uncovered, this Scott wasn't in the position to buy her out, even if he wanted to. So unfortunately, the bottom line was that her land was as essential to him as it was to her. He wanted to build a luxury residential development called Pacific Shores.

Pacific Shores. The thought of covering that beautiful area with more houses and asphalt when it could be used for the good of generations to come lit a fire someplace deep within her.

While on a personal level, she felt sorry for this young man, her supposed half brother, it wouldn't stop her from fighting him—every step of the way.

Tomorrow, she'd rally the troops. Gina said the volunteers were coming in the morning. She'd talk to everyone then.

14

The scenery hadn't changed for miles.

In a move refined over many hours between job sites, Scott Dekker transferred his Starbucks cup to his left hand, kept his car on the road, and tried to find a good station with his right hand.

So far, it was all Toby Keith and Jesus saves. NPR came in, but some liberal was whining about suburban sprawl. Irritated, he turned it off. Obviously they hadn't driven down the I-5 lately. Nothing but cows and trucks for miles. America had plenty of room.

Yes, most of the farmland in the San Joaquin Valley was covered in asphalt and concrete, but so what? He'd been instrumental in paving some of it himself.

Scott was that most hated of Californians, a land developer.

Another green sign with white lettering zipped past. Bakersfield. He couldn't remember the last time he'd been this far south. Most of his business kept him in the Central Valley.

Or used to, when he had business. According to his GPS, Jasper, California, was 162 miles away. Two and a half hours.

He turned his mind to the time he came down here with his mom. She'd surprised him with a trip to Disneyland for his seventh birthday. His favorite ride was Pirates of the Caribbean—floating in on the boat was like entering another universe. So much going on all around him—they went on it three times so they could take it all in. And the fireflies!

Yep, Disneyland was the real thing.

Nothing before or since ever lived up quite so fully to his expectations. Eating corn dogs, nachos, and ice cream. His mom even went on the Matterhorn with him.

He smiled at the memory of his mother, the prim and proper Janet Dekker, blond hair flying out behind her, laughing and shrieking as they hurtled down and around one steep loop after another. He wondered if the Disneyland trip ever surfaced through the fog that clouded her mind the last few years of her life. Alzheimer's probably robbed her even of that.

The next day, she drove them through a narrow canyon to a small beach town to "wiggle our toes in the ocean." Without even checking in to their motel first, they had done just that. Digging in the glove compartment, they found enough quarters for the parking meter, left the Datsun pulled into a narrow space facing the ocean, then went to play in the waves. They even had time to walk down to the tide pools at the foot of a giant rock. He found two sea stars and a baby octopus.

The plan had been to go back again in the morning at low tide—around nine—but the phone rang at seven, and after she talked with whomever was on the other end, his mom said they needed to go. He didn't understand why they had to leave early or why she was so quiet on the ride home. But for once, he didn't pester her with questions. Somehow, he knew better than to ask.

Other than a short vacation to Maui he'd taken with his girlfriend, Scott hadn't left the area since. For college, he commuted to San Jose State. His mom's tiny stucco house in Gilroy was only thirty-five minutes away, without traffic.

Mom was fine back then. It wasn't until after he started working that she began forgetting things. Seven years ago, after several frantic phone calls and late-night emergencies, he started looking into long-term care. The last call he got was from the police. Forgetting something on the stove, his mom then started walking down the street in her nightgown. At some point, she walked into a neighbor's home, thinking it was her own, and became belligerent when they tried to get her to leave.

Facilities that would accept Alzheimer's patients were almost nonexistent, and very expensive. In his prerecession heydays, he could handle the cost and was happy to, after all she'd done for him.

At first, he didn't even notice the extra expense. But when $5,780 a month turned into $9,300 on the Serenity Village bill and the bottom fell out of the market, he wasn't sure how he was going to keep her there. State-run places were out of the question. He'd seen them. And smelled them.

The last five years had been a nightmare. What didn't get wiped out in the crash, he'd used to pay back investors as fairly as possible, before declaring bankruptcy. His partners, older and wiser in the ways of cutthroat capitalism, told him he was a fool. They had long since bailed, leaving him holding the bag. Jodi, the girlfriend he'd taken to Maui, walked out as soon as the money dried up.

Then, last Christmas, his mom died.

A Japanese investor snapped up the Gilroy house, sight unseen. The proceeds were just enough to cover the remainder of the bill at Serenity Village.

Almost rear-ending the BMW in front of him, Scott pulled his attention back to the present and refocused on the road. He spent the next three hours fighting his way through Los Angeles traffic. Around 7:30 p.m., he pulled off at a freeway motel. The rooms were almost as depressing as the exterior. If all went well, this was the last time he'd have to stay in a dump like this.

There was a Denny's across the street, but he was too tired to go out. Polishing off the last of the bag of corn nuts he bought at the gas station, he turned on the TV. He flipped channels for a while but turned it off and stretched out on the bed.

Scott's mind drifted back to the day he went to clear out his mom's house. The day he made the big discovery. He still couldn't believe it. One piece of paper. And it had been there for all those years.

For the seven years his mom was in the home, his property-management people took care of her house for him. Made sure the lawn was mowed, hedges trimmed, and the lights were on a schedule to make it look lived in. False hope or laziness, he wasn't sure which, prevented him from putting it on the market while she was alive.

The night before he had to go through his childhood home, he got good and drunk. He wasn't exactly in great shape that morning. He'd handled huge land deals, managed millions, but this one task overwhelmed him.

To make it easier, he'd given himself a schedule. Trash dumpster in position outside, he'd hired some day laborers to haul everything out. They'd been instructed to show up at 1:00 p.m.

He brought boxes, although he really didn't have room to keep very much, even if he wanted to. The living room was easy. He wasn't into knickknacks, books, or artificial plants. He left all those.

There was a photo wall. His mom had every picture of him since kindergarten up there. Old-school, she displayed her maternal pride on an actual wall, not a virtual one. She was in the home before Facebook became a thing.

He looked at the framed pictures. A baseball game he'd won. Christmas. The first fish he ever caught. A friend's dad had taken him along on a camping trip. He'd been so proud of that fish, a twelve-inch rainbow trout. His mom cleaned and cooked it right then, even though it must have been nine or ten o'clock when he burst in the front door with his prize.

Two rooms later, he hadn't even filled up a third of one box. About noon, he was down to his mom's old, beat-up desk in the corner of her bedroom.

He'd have lunch after this.

Wanting to get through everything as quickly as possible, he opened the solitary file drawer and skimmed the still-brightly-colored labels neatly topping each hanging folder. Mortgage. Utilities. Medical. Taxes. Receipts. Warranties. Manuals. Who kept warranties and manuals? He always threw those out. A quick check of each file yielded old bills, receipts. Nothing he needed to keep.

The last folder was simply labeled "R."

R?

It contained one item, a handwritten letter, addressed to his mother. He read it several times to make sure. Then he just sat there.

He couldn't believe it.

The letter gave him two things: a father and hope for the future. Through guilt or love, a man named Robert not only claimed Scott as his son, but left him a three-mile stretch of pristine oceanfront property in Jasper, California.

Tomorrow, he would see it for the first time.

15

In the last four weeks, Scott hadn't gotten more than five hours of sleep a night, but he'd never felt better. Finally, things were going his way.

The Jasper property went beyond his wildest expectations. Finally, Pacific Shores, a project he'd dreamed about for years but never had the means to develop before the recession, would become a reality.

The ultimate in luxury living, Pacific Shores would have everything the discriminating buyer could desire. Way beyond your typical luxury condominiums, maid, dry cleaning, and gardening services were the least of what residents could expect. Private Pilates, yoga, martial arts, and weight training were also provided—no large, sweaty gym classes here. All personalized and delivered to your door. Dog walkers, masseuses, personal shoppers—Pacific Shore residents would never have to leave their thoughtfully designed units.

He just never had the right piece of property until now.

And when he did find a suitable piece of land, his money was always tied up in other deals. After the crash, he didn't think he'd ever be able to turn those dreams into reality. Now, thanks to this unexpected gift from a father he never knew, he had that chance, and he wasn't about to lose it.

The first thing he'd done after reading the letter was drive down to see the property with his own eyes—to reassure himself the land really existed and wasn't covered in suburban sprawl or a strip mall with a gas station and mini-mart. It did exist, and it was gorgeous! The instant he saw it, he could visualize Pacific Shores. Million-dollar view from each unit, cooling ocean breezes, beautiful artsy town nearby, major shopping within thirty minutes up or down the coast. He still couldn't believe it was his.

Energized for the first time in years, Scott had immediately returned to Milpitas and spent the rest of December customizing his initial plans. Squeezing the last few dollars out of his already-depleted bank account, he had an architect friend draw up some preliminaries and contacted his favorite investors. The problem was, most of his former investors were no longer in business, at least not the business of giving away money.

Except Felix Rodriguez. Not only was he still in the game, but his was just about the *only* game in town. Scott knew him by reputation, and it wasn't stellar. He would get your job done under budget, but only by cutting corners and greasing a few planning inspectors' palms. But beggars can't be choosers.

He read about Rodriguez recently in a trade magazine. One of the publications that kept coming even though he hadn't paid the bill in over a year. It was a rags-to-riches "local boy done good" story.

According to the article, fifty-two-year-old Felix Rodriguez had roots in the Central Valley going back three generations.

Although it didn't come out and say it, the first two were probably undocumented. His grandfather picked fruits and vegetables up and down the West Coast, eventually settling in Gilroy, California, as big agriculture grew. His son, Felix's dad, worked the garlic fields; Felix's mom was a maid. Finally scraping enough money together, with the help of relatives, his parents bought an old, flat-roofed, two-bedroom home when Felix's sister was born. By the look of an old black-and-white picture, it didn't seem like the walls could even support the flimsy roof, let alone provide room enough for six children.

Not afraid of hard labor, the writer said, Felix worked construction from the time he was thirteen years old. By the time he was thirty-five, he grew these skills and two years of college into the most successful construction company in Gilroy. Working toward a degree in geology, the young man had to drop out of school to support the family when his father became too ill with lung cancer to work. Probably from the pesticides, but they didn't mention that in the article, either.

Scott had to grudgingly admit Felix had earned his rags-to-riches credentials. His construction company employed over two hundred people, and photos of his current residence showed a five-thousand-square-foot California split-level over-looking twenty sprawling acres of rolling ranch land.

Felix didn't pound nails anymore.

When Scott heard through the grapevine Felix was flush and looking for projects, he put aside his distaste for the man's reputation and called to set up a meeting.

He needed money. Felix had money. End of story.

Within a week, they had a handshake deal. Within two, a lengthy contract was off to Felix's attorney, Gary Schofield, to do with it whatever it is attorneys do with the mountains of paperwork they deal with every day. The terms were pretty simple. In essence, Scott put up the land; Felix put up the money. They'd split the profits fifty-one–forty-nine, with Scott holding the majority.

A firm down in Southern California would do the actual physical construction. Scott planned to be on-site every day to keep an eye on things. He had no other projects in the Valley and, since his mother had died and his girlfriend had left, no other reason to be there. It was his first project out of the gate after the bankruptcy, and his reputation depended on Pacific Shores living up to the marketing they were about to roll out. He was heading down there this afternoon, meeting with the local architect in the morning. He couldn't wait to see his property again.

Waiting impatiently through Corona del Mar traffic, Scott regretted his decision to take PCH instead of going back up to the 405. Now that he had some cash, he'd decided to treat himself to better accommodations last night and enjoy a leisurely drive down the coast this morning. Well, it was certainly leisurely so far. He'd checked out of the Hyatt in Huntington Beach at 6:30 a.m. Jasper was supposed to be forty-five minutes away, but an hour and a half later, according to his GPS, he was only halfway there.

Idling at a light, Scott noticed the woman in the car next to his, admiring him openly. He was just at the age a man's boyish charm catches up with his experience. It was a good look. Neatly trimmed dark hair, clean shaven, strong jaw. Aviator shades. The woman seemed to particularly enjoy his sexy forearms.

He made it all the way to Jasper's northern city limits before traffic slowed down again. The marine layer was just starting to burn off. His plan was to meet with the architect, then go into town and find a good place to eat. And start scouting for a place to stay. He wanted everything to be perfect.

Finally, he reached Goldenrod and turned right onto the narrow road.

DEVIL'S CLAW

A large sign confronted him on his left. That was weird. Had that sign been there before? Maybe he had the wrong street. The first time he was here, he'd taken the canyon road into town and turned right to get to Goldenrod.

He checked the GPS on his car and on his phone, then squinted back at the street sign. Yes, this was Goldenrod, the road that led to his property. Making sure no one was behind him, he backed up a little and twisted his neck around to reread the large wooden sign he'd passed on his way in.

"Welcome to the Future Home of the Southern Sea Otter Sanctuary and Education Center"

What?

Someone must have posted their sign on the wrong land. But what other land was there? To his left was nothing but a huge pile of black rock that tumbled down into the ocean, where waves crashed uselessly against it. Pretty distinctive feature. Straight ahead, a slim strip of land curved around the top of a bluff that fell two hundred feet down to a small cove, carved out over thousands of years by a patient sea. To the right, the rest of the property—*his* property—stretched for three magnificent miles north.

There was only one road to this land, and he was on it.

There must be some mistake.

Looking back up the road, he saw three large, heavy-duty equipment trucks of some kind on his right, rumbling toward him across the field, kicking up dust. Turning onto the dirt road he was on, about four hundred feet in front of him, they rolled slowly past, toward the highway.

Scott leaned out, trying to catch the attention of one of the drivers. The last truck slowed to an idle behind the first two, waiting for the light, but the driver didn't acknowledge him or roll down his window.

Foot still on the brake, Scott shouted up at him, "Hey, what are you doing here? This is private property."

The driver leaned out as he drove by. "Lunch break—sorry, man!"

It didn't look like they'd hurt anything—nothing had been disturbed that he could see, but still. He wasn't running a parking garage here.

He got back to his main concern. The sign.

Anxiety and anger rising in equal measures, Scott slammed the CLK into park, fumbling for his phone. This was all he needed.

16

FEBRUARY 2015

His first call got dropped. He'd have to find a way to boost cell phone signals out here. He tried again. This time a young girl cheerfully answered.

"Rodriguez Construction. How may I help you today?"

"Felix Rodriguez, please." His knee started pumping up and down.

"Yes, sir. He's about to go into a meeting. Who should I say is calling?"

"Tell him it's Scott. Scott Dekker."

"Oh, hello, Mr. Dekker. Hold on, I'll see if I can catch him before he goes in."

While he waited, he backed up to the sign, took a picture, then sent it to himself for backup. Phone and website were included helpfully on the bottom of the sign. If he wanted to donate, he was to contact anyone at Friends of the Sea Otter.

The girl came back on the line. "He'll be right with you, Mr. Dekker. He said he'd take your call in his office."

Ocean waves provided a soothing soundtrack, but Scott felt anything but relaxed. An aggressive seagull dive-bombed him. Irritated, he pushed a button, and the black cloth top, unfolding itself, began to smoothly rise. When it was up, he flicked the levers shut to secure it. Rolled up the windows. Much better. He couldn't hear anything anyway, with those damn waves pounding in the background.

"Scott. What's up? You there already?" Felix asked.

"Yeah, I'm here, but there's a problem. You ever hear of something called the Southern Sea Otter Sanctuary and Education Center or an organization called Friends of the Sea Otter?"

"No, why? Did someone hit you up for a donation?"

Scott allowed himself a cynical smile. "No, no, they didn't hit me up for a donation, but they've put a fence up on my property and are announcing their intention to build on it."

Felix was quiet, then said, "Must be some mistake. Are you in the right place? Is there a number on the sign or a website or any contact info?" His voice remained calm.

Scott forwarded him the information and waited while Felix went to find somebody to take his meeting.

Up to this point, everything had gone so well. He should have known. Nothing was ever this easy. At least, nothing in his life.

Felix came back on the line. He asked Scott to go over the details again.

Scott did, then waited. Whatever the solution was, it would take money. Money was the solution to every problem. Scott didn't have any, and they both knew it.

Not wanting to ask, he waited for Felix to offer.

After a silence a beat longer than it needed to be, he did.

"Look, let's not worry about it yet. I'll have Gary look into it. He's down in Orange County, working on another deal for me. Hopefully he can get it cleared up in a day or two."

"Yeah, okay," Scott said, relieved.

Felix *should* offer to help. When wealthy Californians started claiming their piece of this extremely rare Pacific Shores paradise, Felix was going to make a bundle. It was in his best interest to help.

"Yeah, cancel the architect . . . tell him something came up, you'll reschedule. Don't give him details." Then he added, in a lighter, more cheerful tone, "How's the CLK handling? You enjoying it?"

"It's great, Felix," Scott said, wishing he'd brought his own car now. Felix never missed the opportunity to let him know who held the financial reins.

"Don't worry, Scott. This'll turn out to be nothing. See you in the morning. Oh, and bring all your paperwork—Gary's probably going to need notarized copies of everything," Felix said, "Cherie can fax them."

The drive back to Milpitas wasn't nearly as much fun as the drive down.

◦ ◦ ◦ ◦ ◦

Alone in his office, Felix sat in his captain's chair and stared out a large picture window. Not much of a view. Unless you were into employee parking lots. A large map of California took up most of the other wall to the left of his desk. A water cooler squatted near San Diego. The rest of the room was typical of a contractor's office. Couple of sturdy visitor chairs. Dark-brown leather chesterfield along the wall, just long enough for thinking naps. His secretary knew not to bother him between one and two.

No need to panic yet.

Hopefully, Gary would get everything cleared up quickly.

Confusion over landownership happened more often than people thought. Usually, it was just a matter of misfiled paperwork. People were lazy. Sometimes they didn't register the title.

If this sea otter place thought they had a claim and it turned into a formal dispute, there were ways of dealing with that. Besides, if those two years of geology were worth anything, he had more than one way of making money off this property. He'd know more when he got the report from the thumper trucks. Bill always paid extra for a positive report.

Pushing himself up out of his chair, he walked from behind his desk to stand in front of the map. At five ten, he stood eye level with San Francisco. Full head of hair. No gray yet. Hard muscles lurking beneath a few extra pounds, Felix had the solid build of a man who could, but no longer did, haul drywall.

He ran his hand along the surface of the map, causing his new Rolex to glint briefly in the sun. Large brown eyes contemplated the lines, letters, and colors. This was the original—the one he'd used when he started Rodriguez Construction—a tangible display of his accomplishments. For the most part, Cherie kept it updated. Current projects marked with blue pins, completed projects with green.

"Green for money," he told her with a wink.

Most of the pins clumped together in the middle of the state, demonstrating his domination of the Santa Clara County construction market.

Recently, a scattering of clear ones had appeared. He placed those himself. Only he knew what they represented. And what they represented was big bucks. Today, he made sure the one located in Jasper, California, was securely pushed in, right next to a blue one.

One or both of those pins was going to pay for Mia's tuition at Stanford Law. His niece's goal was to sit on the Supreme

Court someday. Sotomayor was her hero. She'd probably do it, too. If he could keep her in school.

Somebody always needed something. Helping someone up from Mexico, starter homes for most of the kids. And there were a lot of kids. The Rodriguez brood was always growing—must have been over fifty relatives at Yolanda's quinceañera last month. His cousin Jared, thirty-two years old, had five kids already. Whenever he objected to having another one, his wife just laughed.

"Just doing my part, honey. We're taking California back . . . one baby at a time!" she said.

Felix remembered his first job in construction. His boss never bothered to learn their names. It was always "Hey, Jose . . ." A man of truly limited vocabulary. "Dirty Mexicans!" or "Damn Mexicans!" is how he referred to them as a whole, even though half of the guys were from Guatemala.

Idiot.

Pressing both pins firmly into the wall again with his thumb, he returned to his desk. He had two phone calls to make.

17

Since it was a holiday, the place was deserted. Scott had no trouble following the receptionist's directions to conference room B. It was the only one with lights on.

Felix remained seated at the small conference table and made introductions. The attorney, Gary Schofield, reached across to shake hands. Scott sat at the only other chair available. Felix refreshed his mug of coffee from the carafe in the center of the table and nodded for the attorney to begin.

He had never met Felix's attorney before. In a suit that hung on a tall but bony frame, the attorney had a long face and droopy eyes that reminded Scott of a morose bloodhound suffering from insomnia. He hoped he had some good news, but the man looked as if he regularly swam in a pool of bad news and was about to deliver some of it to Scott.

At least he was quick about it.

For a moment, no one said anything. Finally, Scott spoke.

"You're kidding" was all he could manage.

Gary grimaced a smile and, with one large hand, slid the pertinent documents smoothly over to Scott.

"See for yourself."

"I have a sister?" Scott said.

"Half sister," Gary corrected, surprised this was Scott's first comment.

"And she says she owns my land?" Scott said.

Gary nodded.

"But what about the sea otter sanctuary? It's already all but built! How can she build on my land!"

Felix let Gary continue to answer Scott's questions.

"She donated the use of the land to a foundation she started. Technically the foundation built it. It's still hers. It's complicated."

Scott's mind reeled. Years of working hard and doing the right thing. Inheriting this land was the first good thing that had happened to him in the last eight years. He thought he'd finally caught a break. And now this.

He abruptly stood up, then sat back down. Raking his fingers through his hair, he leaned in, anger rising to replace shock.

"She can't give away my land! What proof does she have? Did you show her the letter? Doesn't that prove I own it?"

"Yes, along with the handwriting verification. We sent copies of everything to her attorney. Your father was an artist—fairly well-known in his day. Lots of handwriting samples available. The graphologist was certain. No one's really contesting that. It's considered a holographic will—it's in his handwriting all right, dated and signed. It should stand up in court—in California you don't need witnesses for a holographic will," Gary said.

"Then what's the problem? Why isn't that enough evidence that this piece of property belongs to me?"

"Because, being the only living heir—the only one anyone knew about," he added, "she was given all her father's property when he died, completely legally, including lot 429. Since neither of you tried to sell the property before now, the issue of title never came up. No one knew about you."

Felix nodded for Gary to wrap it up.

"Unless we can convince her to release her claim, which I highly doubt—she hasn't budged so far—you'll have to fight it out in court," Gary said.

Scott fumed, unable to absorb this news fully.

Twenty years ago he would have been excited to learn he had a sister, even a half sister, but not today.

What he felt today was sick. He didn't have the resources to fight it out in court. Or the time. He'd be broke and his dream project scuttled long before anything could be settled. Who was he kidding? He was already broke. The land was all he had. And he'd need an all-out win, completely clear title to the land, with no financial losses. He was going to have to make a deal with the devil.

Felix.

Now that the situation had been made clear to Scott, Felix entered the conversation. He had to make sure Scott was good and scared before he threw him a lifeline.

Felix's manner was casual, as if this were nothing but a hiccup. "I think it's worth it," he said. "We can fight this. Gary thinks our chances are good."

Scott looked up. He said "we." A wave of relief swept through him. That meant Felix was in. Pacific Shores wasn't lost yet. They'd have to demolish and remove the other building, but that could be done without too much expense. He did wish she hadn't built it. It would make her claim stronger on the property, Gary explained.

Now all he needed to know was exactly what Felix's help would cost him. He wouldn't accept favors, and he knew Felix never gave anything away.

He was correct.

After Gary gave him an estimate, depending on how long it dragged out, Scott gave up additional shares in Pacific Shores. That made him and Felix equal partners now. Gary said he'd do some more digging, see what possible negotiating points they could come up with. In the meantime, he'd draw up a new contract with appropriate language, reflecting their oral agreement, taking into account any contingencies or extra expenses incurred. It'd be ready in a few days.

The contract may have already been drawn up. Then Felix could wait for a few days, just to make it look good, before having Gary's office sending it out for signatures. They knew Scott had no choice.

"We need to ramp things up a little, Scott," Felix said.

"What do you mean?"

"It's time for you to get out front and center on this thing. Gary will handle the legal side of things. We need you to make your case with the community—make your side sympathetic."

"Like how?"

"Your half sister understands—she's been busy."

Felix spread some brochures and press releases on the table. "Not only did she get her center built in record time, she's been showing up at every council meeting, Eagle Scout ceremony, and kids' science camp program, mainly through that director of hers . . ." He turned the bottom of the press release around to look at the bottom. "Gina Richardson, drumming up public support for this Southern Sea Otter Sanctuary."

Scott still didn't know what he had in mind. He couldn't see himself at an Eagle Scout meeting, and he wasn't a public speaker.

"You need to get out there," Felix said, pulling out his phone, checking his calendar. "There's a city council meeting July 13. Gary got us on the agenda."

"Why even bother? Everyone's going to love the furry little sea otter and a local celebrity artist more than a land developer," Scott said.

"They don't know about the contested title," Gary said. "They've supported the Southern Sea Otter Sanctuary so far— the majority of the board are environmentally inclined—but more than half of those people are small-business owners. A town like Jasper depends on tax revenue. You can make the case that your development would bring in a lot more tax dollars and business for the town."

The last few months had been extremely frustrating, not being able to do anything toward resolving this problem. He couldn't build Pacific Shores and had no other projects to work on. Scott was barely scraping by financially. He could do this. He had to do this.

Meeting over, the men stood. Gary gathered his papers, snapped his briefcase shut, and pushed in his chair. As he walked into the hallway, he turned back.

"On the bright side, Scott, Solange Sauvage is old. We drag this out long enough . . ."

Felix chuckled.

Man, these guys are heartless.

But then, given the battle he was facing, heartless is what he needed. He couldn't afford to let the possibility of some kind of kumbaya moment of family reunion with a newly discovered half sister even enter his brain.

Focus.

Focus helped him survive the chaos of the last five years, and focus would see him through this. On the drive home in the car, he began to feel somewhat more hopeful. He could do this. He had to do this.

By the time he got to his computer, so many ideas came tumbling out, his speech was practically writing itself.

18

Felix slipped up behind his wife, kissing her on the neck on his way to the fridge for a beer.

"Querida mia."

This morning's meeting had gone well, and he was home in time for the holiday.

Celia bumped him away with her hip.

"Smells great," he said, leaning over the large pot of posole she was stirring.

He looked around the kitchen. Good thing he put in that island. The women had filled every square inch of counter space. Everyone brought their specialties. Gorditas de chorizo; several different kinds of flautas with avocado cream, lime, shredded lettuce, and sliced radishes on the side; rice; beans; watermelon chunks; fresh tortillas; mango aqua fresca. Flan, Jell-O, and trays of cookies and cupcakes for dessert. Tequila for the *tios*. Lots of beer.

Fourth of July was an odd holiday for Mexicans to celebrate, he thought, but the kids liked the fireworks. His house was on a hill, so you could see the colorful display from the wrap-around, second-floor deck better than you could see it in town. When the sun went down, everyone would be dragging their chairs up there to watch the show.

People had been arriving all day. As he made his way up the stairs, he greeted several and looked out through the living room windows to the backyard. Most of the kids were in the pool. Young mothers kept a sharp eye on them from the shade. One grandmother leaned over to an infant, lightly tapping the top and bottom lips of a particularly adorable baby, crooning, *"Da me una sonrisa!"*

The baby obliged, and all the women laughed.

More women's voices drifted up from the kitchen. He could hear them rising and falling, talking about food, kids, and, sometimes, their men, most of whom were in the den, anchoring couches and La-Z-Boys, beers in hand, eyes glued to the game. Soccer today, not baseball. He loved the sound of women's voices.

Walking through the master bedroom, Felix let himself out onto the private balcony and checked the thermometer on the side of the house. One hundred ten degrees. Dressed for the heat in khakis and a cotton shirt, he sat at a wrought-iron cafe table tucked into an alcove. Looking out on the valley, he enjoyed the view and thought about smoking a cigar. Celia didn't like them in the house.

He had just about decided to go inside and get one when his phone rang. It was Bill.

"Hey," he said, taking a long pull of his beer, then rolled the cold bottle across his forehead.

"Felix, Bill here. How's your Fourth?"

"Good. You? You going to watch any fireworks?"

"Yeah, we always do the boat parade. Maureen's folks have a place near the water."

Felix kept up the friendship charade. Bill always pretended they were friends. Equals. But Felix knew better. Nancy's folks lived in San Francisco. The "near the water" location Bill casually mentioned meant a multimillion-dollar Victorian right on the bay.

Bill worked for Ester Oil, a subsidiary of a major oil company whose name you'd recognize. Felix and Bill had been doing business now for about two years, and so far, the arrangement had been mutually profitable.

After a few more minutes of small talk, Bill got to the point.

"So, what's the news? You got anything good for me?" he asked. He sounded tense. Bill always sounded tense.

"I might," Felix said.

He so enjoyed keeping Bill on the hook. He'd had the results from the thumper trucks in Jasper since February, before the Southern Sea Otter Center was even built.

"Oakland was a bust—nothing substantial there. Nothing worth your time. Too deep. Too scattered. But I got a good preliminary report back from that property in Jasper."

He didn't want to tell him how good yet.

"Okay, good. When can I get the final?" Bill's voice relaxed a little.

"I'll send it as soon as I get it."

"You sure these guys are reliable? I don't like having this many fingers in the pie." Bill's voice ratcheted up a notch.

"I'm paying them enough money—no reason for them to talk," Felix said. "Not in their best interest. Besides, you recommended them in the first place. We had to have someone who knew how to run those things. I can't use my guys." He was getting tired of Bill worrying about things all the time.

"Okay. Let me know if we need to bump up their money," Bill said.

And take more of my share? "No, they're okay."

He was paying the experienced drivers under the table, not Bill. As usual, he took all the risks. Bill could always claim he had nothing to do with the trucks exploring for oil without permits. But Felix wasn't too worried anyone would even notice. To the general public, the trucks looked like any other construction vehicles driving in and around empty lots in residential Orange County. Each thumping session didn't take very long, could be done in the morning hours, and the drivers knew to play dumb if anyone asked what they were doing.

With a few more assurances and wishes for a safe holiday, he got Bill off the phone.

Felix slowly pushed his thumbnail straight up through the label on the sweating bottle. Once clear, it fell onto the table, rolled into a perfect curve, quickly drying in the hot air.

He knew Bill from college. They had been in a lot of the same classes. After Felix had to drop out to help his family, Bill went on to graduate, landing a good job at Ester. No surprise there—unless you taught college, nobody else was hiring geology majors but the oil companies. It was still that way.

Bill came from Boston bluebloods. They didn't exactly run in the same circles, so Felix was surprised one morning a couple years ago when Cherie said a Mr. Bill Stanton was on the line. The minute he heard Bill's voice, he remembered him. Always tapping a pencil or shifting his feet, Bill was never at rest. He wondered what he wanted.

They met up for lunch at Red Lyon. It took Bill about twenty-five minutes to get to the point.

Ester specialized in oil exploration and production. Bill's job was on the exploration end. He managed both the Central and Southern California land regions. Someone else did offshore. That's where the new money was, but with new ways of finding and extracting it, there was still enough interest to meet Bill's needs.

Settling in over his Monte Cristo, he explained how in the early days, his job had been easy. Oil was everywhere. But most of the easy-to-find sources in California had been tapped out. There was still oil, but it was deeper or harder extract. That's why fracking became popular.

"People want oil, but they don't want us to do what we need to do to get it out of the ground," he said between bites. "If you could just stick a pipe in there and suck up some black gold, well, it'd be great!" Bill said, his two-olive gin martini—very James Bond—loosening him up. "But that's not the case anymore."

Felix made encouraging noises.

"And the friends of the spotted owl or the striped polar bear or whatever the animal of the week is make it almost *impossible* for me to do my job! There are so many regulatory agencies to go through it costs a fortune and takes years sometimes just to send a couple of thumper trucks in there to see if there's anything worth drilling for."

He took a healthy slug of his drink, placing it somewhat askew on the cocktail napkin.

Felix was beginning to get the picture.

"And here's the kicker. We've already bent over backward to please these leeches. Developed new technologies that have less of an environmental impact. Hell, the thumper trucks aren't even real thumper trucks anymore. The environmentalists were worried we'd knock little birdies out of their nests or wake up some groundhogs. Lucky for us, the new technology works. The new thumper trucks just park, weight drop, vibrate, and read the signals that bounce back up.

"You know how it works—different waves indicate water, rock, shale, and the mother lode—oil. We can still find the stuff. We just have to get permission to get the trucks in there. There just aren't a lot of big empty tracts of land to check out anymore. The easy pickings are gone. Now we've got to see what's under and around people's houses and businesses. No one wants us there."

Felix could see what Bill was getting around to.

"That's where you come in," Bill said, wiping his mouth with the large linen napkin, pushing his plate back a bit, which the waiter swooped in to spirit away.

The rest of their conversation was conducted in quieter tones. After clearing the table, the waiter brought an additional round of drinks. Bill didn't notice he was on his third martini, while Felix was only on his second beer.

By the end of their lunch, they'd hammered out the details of their agreement, which, when he sobered up the next day, Bill surely realized favored Felix a bit more than he'd originally planned. No formal contract. Nothing in writing. Bill needed a way to save his boss the time and expense of getting permission and holding public meetings in order to send thumper trucks in to see if there was any oil worth digging for. This way, Ester could go in knowing the oil was already there.

The company would still have to jump through various local, state, and federal hoops, but it was a huge head start and made him look clairvoyant to the higher-ups.

Bill had explained how it worked. His bosses looked the other way. His educated guesses would easily translate into bonuses and promotions. The pittance he paid Felix was nothing compared to how much he would benefit. And he wanted the money—he was over this job. His father was one of those stalwart "make it on your own" men, so after college, he was on his own.

Felix, the largest contractor in the area, with several satellite offices, had continual access to pieces of property being developed. Civilians wouldn't notice a few more big equipment trucks coming and going, and the workers, who would know right away they weren't construction trucks, would turn a blind eye if they wanted to keep their jobs.

Win-win. It had worked well. Bill slipped Felix a monthly retainer. Felix sent in a couple of trucks at unobtrusive times. When they found something, which wasn't often—most of the oil had already been discovered—Felix passed the information along to Bill. He made sure the reports came to him first. He didn't want Bill stiffing him. Every positive report resulted in a bonus for both of them, although Bill's bonus was five times bigger than what he parceled out to Felix. The company, of course, didn't know anything about Felix.

Once he knew there was enough oil to bother with, Bill went through all the hoops to get official permissions to "explore." Whether the oil company wound up needing to buy the land or mineral rights eventually didn't matter to Felix. He made his money on the front end. Bill looked like Nostradamus to the higher-ups in the oil company, and Felix got his bank accounts fattened.

Bill had a lot more to lose than Felix did. But the rewards were so much greater than the risks, it was an easy decision for both of them.

Felix sipped his beer.

Bill was going to shit his pants when he saw this report. He'd been sitting on it since February, waiting to see how the title dispute turned out. He may have to double his fee for this one. How this much oil in one concentrated pool had escaped previous detection, he had no idea. He finished his beer and went back inside.

He thought about his options.

If the title court upheld Scott's claim to lot 429, Felix would put up the money to build Pacific Shores, and get most of the profit. That was the above-board deal. Good money and it wouldn't take long. Properties like that sold quickly. And that didn't preclude his doing a simultaneous deal with Bill. That was totally separate.

He would get his fat bonus cash from Bill for passing along the thumper truck report, making Bill's bosses happy. Once he had both those chunks of money, he didn't care what happened to the infamous lot 429. Build, demo, drill—it was all the same to him.

The only fly in the ointment was this sea otter center. But all was not lost. It was just a matter of timing. He just had to keep Bill from finding out about it until after he collected his finder's fee for the oil pool.

Bill would pull the plug on everything if he found out about the sea otter center. With an environmental nature center for an endangered species sitting on it, the oil company would never be able to touch that land, let alone drill for oil there. Even if the oil company could bribe their way past the government gatekeepers, the public outcry for the cute little sea otter would effectively kill any deal they could make.

Of course, with this much oil, Ester might decide to buy an adjacent lot and drill sideways right under the center and just ride out any complaints.

But Felix knew Bill. He'd back out if he caught wind of any complications. No deal, no payday for Felix.

The only thing that could screw up his plans now was the sea otter center. He hadn't been able to prevent it from being built, but hopefully, his most recent efforts would prevent it from ever opening.

19

SATURDAY, JULY 4, 2015

Felix could be such an asshole. Who did he think he was? Being greedy got you caught. When this last deal was done, maybe he'd pull the plug. He didn't need Felix.

Greasy Mexican.

Seeing the time, Bill loosened his tie, tossed a file into his inbox, and pulled on his jacket, dropping his keys into the front pocket. He even left his laptop. He could get Felix's report on his phone. That was the only file he planned on opening this weekend. Once he and Rhonda checked in at the hotel, he was off the clock.

All work and no play makes Jack a dull boy.

But first, he had to check the wife box. Maureen expected him at La Folie at 7:00 p.m. sharp. Her parents were in town. That meant hearing all about their latest trip to Europe. The evening ahead held all the appeal of wet sand recently visited by a cat. He closed his office door more firmly than necessary, engaging the automatic lock.

"Night, Bill! Have anything fun planned?"

His secretary, Sally Monahan, whose desk was right outside his office, looked up as she turned off her computer and quickly pulled her purse out of a bottom drawer, gathering her things to go. They were the only two left on this floor.

"Meeting the wife for dinner in the city," Bill said, not stopping to chat.

"Sounds like fun!" she said to the back of his head as he continued walking.

He nodded, heading for the elevator without bothering to ask if she needed him to walk her to her car. The parking lot was not well lit. Last year one, of the girls in accounting had been raped on her way out.

Once inside the elevator, he pressed "P," waving aimlessly back at her as the door closed.

At least he had the Porsche. With his new promotion, the one his wife didn't know about, he could have afforded more but didn't want to draw attention to his new windfalls, or listen to his father-in-law tell him to invest in the stock market instead. As if that ever helped anyone. His father-in-law was *always* giving him financial advice. What did he know, anyway? He had all his money given to him, along with being born with a silver spoon in his mouth. Bill's family may have been able to claim they came over on the *Mayflower*, but Maureen's folks owned the ship. They had the real money.

For years, that had been enough for him to put up with her snide, supercilious attitude. Maureen equated big wallets with big brains, and when Bill had failed to deliver the goods, she sadly accepted her poor decision in the matrimonial department. She didn't file for divorce.

"Van Burens don't do divorce."

Instead, she got very busy with her committees and firmly but politely placed him on a separate shelf. A bottom shelf. One marked "loser." He felt her condescension every Goddamn day.

But not anymore. It used to eat him up, but he was amazed at how little it bothered him since Rhonda came along. Rhonda with the open heart and smile. Rhonda with the long legs and little brain. Just thinking about her perfect breasts made him hard.

He floored the gas pedal and passed several cars. The sooner he got there, the sooner this evening would be over and he could get on the road to Napa. For New Year's, when Maureen went to her spa, Rhonda found them a great little B and B. It had become their place. Just like in the movies, the owners remembered their names and always welcomed them with open arms, making sure he had extra pillows and Rhonda had her pom juice and peanut butter cups. Rhonda did not need to diet.

He told Maureen he had a conference to attend. She didn't even pretend to mind anymore. He knew she wouldn't want to come.

Maureen hadn't come in years.

He checked his watch. Being late was another Van Buren no-no. Nothing to be done, though. He'd just have to endure his father-in-law's judgmental frown. Traffic always slowed down around the Embarcadero.

Bill checked his chin in the rearview mirror. Pulled out an electric razor from the glove compartment for a quick shave.

Maybe he should pull the plug. He almost had enough squirreled away. He'd love to cut Felix loose and be done with that whole arrangement.

He didn't need much to keep Rhonda happy. Unlike Maureen, who required annual shopping trips to Paris and increasingly prolonged stays at an exclusive spa in Palm Springs, Rhonda was not high maintenance. Like an eager puppy, she squealed with delight at the smallest gift. For her birthday, he'd surprised her with a pair of small diamond earrings, a gift Maureen wouldn't have deemed worthy to give the maid.

You'd have thought he'd given her the moon. To thank him, Rhonda walked around in nothing but the earrings for most of the rest of the weekend. Quite a return on his investment.

He doubted his father-in-law would approve.

20

"**M**orning, you guys are here early," Gina greeted Amy, Jeff, and Logan with a smile. The trio was just getting off the elevator.

Liam was taking the afternoon shift today. Dennis was back and insisted on working, but Gina said she felt better having someone work with him. The ER doctor kept him overnight, ran him through some tests, but said overall he'd been lucky. He hadn't sustained any lasting damage. All he had to show for the explosion was a three-inch square bald spot, a few stitches, and a large square gauze bandage. The police said there had been two devices. Probably meant to go off at the same time but set by amateurs, so there was a delay. Dennis said when he heard the first explosion, he took the elevator up to see what was going on. The second went off just as he got to the lobby.

Seated at the stainless steel island in the center of the lab, Gina looked up from her laptop.

Hanging her fringed leather purse on one of the wall hooks

near the door as she walked in, Amy took one of the black ponchos, slipped it on over her T-shirt and jeans, and grabbed a welder's mask off the shelf above. Jeff did the same.

Logan wasn't going to be working directly with Otter 1 today, so she didn't have to put on the Darth Vader outfit. They were hot and clumsy to work in, so she couldn't say she was terribly disappointed, although she loved grooming and feeding Otter 1. How could you not fall in love with the beautiful little sea creature when those sparkling black eyes looked up at you with intelligent curiosity?

"Hi, Gina—we wanted to get a start. This is Sa—I mean, Otter 1's diving debut, right?" Amy said.

"Well, not diving yet, that will have to wait for a surrogate mom, if we get that far, but yes, today's her first day in the pool. Want to carry her down?"

"Yes!"

Gina didn't have to ask Amy twice.

The large viewing area of the aquarium was upstairs, off the lobby, separate from the newborn tank on level 2. That's where the public would be able to watch and learn about southern sea otters. Rocks made to look like the natural ones in the cove below, a resting platform with ice-chip beds, and a pool that curved around in front all made for maximum otter viewing.

One floor down, on level 2, where they were now, was where most of the behind-the-scenes work took place—it contained Gina's lab, the newborn tank, an oil-spill cleanup room, two small offices, and an exit leading to the employee parking lot on the south end of the facility.

The only natural light on this level came from a pair of floor-to-ceiling sliding doors in the back right corner of the lab. Whenever possible, these were left open to let in sunshine and fresh air. There was an elevator, but everyone preferred to use the long set of metal stairs that zigzagged down to get to level 1, where the training pool was. It was faster, at least until their charge became too heavy to carry easily.

Tucked back into the curve of the building, level 1 contained the above-ground swimming pool where Otter 1, with the help of her Star Wars accomplices, was going to learn how to be an otter.

While waiting for Gina to finish what she was doing, Logan walked through the lab and out onto the small metal landing deck, which stuck out from the building about five feet. From this vantage point, she could see directly down to the training pool, which was only steps away from the cove below. Gina said that even though the otter pool on the lower level was separated from the waves crashing onto the rocks, for the safety of the trainers, they had built it ten feet higher than the small crescent of rocky beach framing the cove. Without that extra height, a good storm surge could sweep the training pool right into the Pacific.

Jeff offered to let Amy be the one to carry the otter pup. She'd put in more hours than he had. It was only fair.

While the kids were suiting up, getting ready to load Otter 1 into her carrier, Gina called Logan over and showed her the data she needed entered into the computer. It looked pretty straightforward. They tracked everything from supplies to how much Otter 1 ate, had grown, and weighed. They also tracked her accomplishments, like hauling out, paddling, and, soon, diving.

"Can we get her now?" Amy asked.

"Sure, go ahead, she can haul herself out now," Gina said. "I'll be right there, just need to finish this up."

When Amy left the room, Gina turned to Logan.

"You are aware that Jeff has a major crush on your daughter, right?"

Logan rolled her eyes. She had definitely noticed. You'd have to be deaf, dumb, and blind not to see the lovelorn puppy eyes he made at Amy every time she entered the room.

She didn't like to butt in, but she'd have to talk to Amy about it soon. Jeff was such a sweet kid, she didn't want to see him get hurt. The other day, a few lines of a song he was writing—something about the sun glinting off silky strands of fair hair and falling into deep, green eyes drifted up the stairs from the recording studio to her office. Yep—it was definitely time to have a talk with the boy.

Gina completed the seafood order she'd been working on and hit "Send," then gave up her stool to Logan.

"It's a good thing we're going to get some more exposure at that city council meeting," Gina said. "We sure need the money. Even one little otter eats a lot, and if things continue to go well, we'll have another one soon—I got a call from La Jolla. Another stranding. Male. Not a pup. We're seeing more migrate down . . . We need to be ready."

"When is the meeting?" Amy asked as they walked by. "Can Liam and I or Jeff say something?"

Gina donned her own Darth Vader gear. "The meeting's next Monday night, and yes, I think anyone can speak at a city council meeting. You just have to get there early and sign up for a three-minute slot. They ostensibly want to hear from the public." Gina rolled her eyes.

"You're speaking, right?" Amy asked.

"Yes—we're on the program. Solange asked me to do the presentation, which will be followed by public comments. The city council members have been pretty supportive, but I don't trust any politicians, even local ones. We need to get the word out there every chance we get. That land developer Scott Dekker's going to speak, too," she said. "He may win some of them over. Supposedly he has proof Solange's dad is also his father, and he left that piece of property to him in a handwritten letter."

They had all been surprised when Solange told them about the title dispute, but no one wanted to quit, even after the attack on the center that put Dennis in the hospital. He was the first one to volunteer to keep going.

"You can't let those guys win," he said.

He reasoned that if they had wanted to hurt people, they would have blown up the lower level, where everyone knew Gina and Dennis worked. They agreed this was just a scare tactic. They hadn't planned on one of the explosives going off late just when Dennis came up to investigate.

If anything, this attempt to intimidate Solange into not opening the center and help the sea otters made everyone feel more determined to stay on and work harder. Once they were open and the community saw how valuable they were, it would be harder for the land developer to win in court. Or so they hoped.

Amy looked anxious.

"Well, what if the land turns out to be his?" she asked. "What will happen to this place?"

"We'll have to cross that bridge when we come to it, but as of now, Solange has title, free and clear," Gina said. "So we have to have our ducks in a row. We've got to convince the city council not to withdraw their support for this project. My main goal is to explain why we need this center, why they made the right decision in the first place. We need to keep people on our side."

"You'll do great, Gina!" Amy said, her voice rising. "We have the right on our side! We have *tons* of houses and hotels and things." She waved her arms vaguely inland, encompassing all of Southern California. "What we *don't* have is a place to help sea otters!"

Listening to Amy, Logan hoped people would see things her way, but understood how easily public opinion could be swayed. People were sheep.

And money talked. Things could go either way.

21

Most real estate titles were fee simple absolute, but if there was one thing Gary knew, it was that the law was rarely simple and never absolute. If it were, people wouldn't need attorneys like him. Everything was open to interpretation. Whoever had the better lawyer and the most money won.

Gary loved not having any skin in the game. Win or lose, his fee was paid. That's why he was sitting here in a beige room indistinguishable from a thousand other bland, bureaucratic rooms, laboring with other clerks and attorneys under eye-straining fluorescent lights, hunched over long tables and uncomfortable plastic bucket chairs, methodically digging through records.

His mission? Establish clear title for lot 429. Lot 429, now located at the intersection of Pacific Coast Highway and Goldenrod, a piece of coastal property in Jasper, California, in which Felix had invested heavily with Scott Dekker, the young man who had inherited it—or thought he had.

Having drawn up the paperwork, Gary knew all the details. Scott put up the land, and Felix put up the cash to build Scott's dream project, Pacific Shores, a luxury residential development right on the beach. Each home would sell for millions. If Solange's title was upheld, they both stood to lose.

Scott had the most to lose, though, as the bulk of Felix's financial commitment to the project came with the build-out of Pacific Shores, which could not be started until the title issue was resolved.

Felix rubbed his eyes and pushed his elbows back to squeeze out the tension between his shoulder blades. He thought about the merits of Scott's case.

Scott's claim to ownership was fairly strong, as claims go. He had a one-hundred-percent handwritten letter from his biological father giving him the property. His father's name was not on his birth certificate, but there was a family resemblance. And DNA testing had been used in other probate cases to establish a high probability a half-sibling relationship existed.

This letter, which Scott hoped would be accepted by the court as a holographic will, met many of the requirements for authenticity. It was dated, signed, and contained an unambiguous description of the property and the owner's intent to leave it to his illegitimate son.

Of course, Gary knew that truth had nothing to do with it. There would be a lengthy court battle, but this Solange wasn't a starving artist. It would just be a matter of whose pockets were deeper, hers or Felix's.

Gary's job was to look for any irregularities that would bolster their case and save them the time and expense of a long, drawn-out battle. Most title disputes were settled out of court. Two years and one-hundred-thousand dollars was the current average for a case to come to trial in Orange County

Superior Court. Felix could swing it but wasn't one to spend money if he didn't have to.

For convenience, Gary got a room at the Courtyard Marriott on Jamboree Road in Irvine, just down from the main Orange County courthouse. He hadn't been down to Southern California for a while and forgot that probate court was in downtown Santa Ana, a good ten miles and sometimes over an hour away with traffic.

Once he'd parked and made his way through the crush of jurists, bailiffs, and other attorneys, he checked in and asked the clerk, out of curiosity, why the probate court wasn't located with the main courthouse. The tiny Asian woman, who for some reason had dyed her bangs a bright mermaid blue, informed him frankly that the county had run out of money before they could complete the build-out of the ancillary courts in that location.

Brilliant.

He hoped this wouldn't take more than a few days.

Felix put him on the job just after he got the call from Scott.

Felix wanted this problem solved.

Yesterday.

Gary knew Felix had more than just a real estate deal to protect. Although Felix thought he'd covered his tracks, Gary knew all about the thumper trucks and the "bonuses" his friend Bill from the oil company slipped him for tips about where to drill for oil. He knew how Felix stood to benefit not only from the sale of Pacific Shores, but from these extra influxes of cash. He had to admit—Felix positioned himself well. He was set to make money twice off this land, if he timed it right.

As soon as Pacific Shores was built and sold and Felix had his money safely in the bank, he'd give Bill the green light and the oil company would swoop in and "explore" for the oil Bill already knew was there.

The amount of oil sitting under lot 429 was enough for Ester to risk the bad publicity of disturbing a few sea otters. If Solange lost the title dispute, Scott and Felix would build their luxury residential development. All Ester would have to do then was purchase a neighboring lot, drill down, and go in sideways, right under the feet of the wealthy residents of Pacific Shores.

Gary didn't much care. He was getting paid either way. He got back to work.

Title searches were unglamorous. He'd been at it for hours now, holed up in this basement, painstakingly documenting the chain of title. Other than his left eye twitching from fatigue, he didn't mind the drab task.

In fact, he was beginning to enjoy it. He'd picked up the scent. Something was not quite right—there was an unexplained gap. Gary's heart beat a little faster.

He had always enjoyed the hunt. The elusive detail, the one illuminating fact or unknown court case that would strengthen his argument. The law, after all, was all about arguments. Whoever had the better lawyer. Justice had nothing to do with it.

In the last few years, Felix had so much work for him, he'd become something of a specialist in land law. Not only had this proved lucrative, but this narrow field of practice suited his solitary nature.

Gary held the ignorant masses in distinct disdain. Few members of the general public appreciated the nuanced layers and precise definitions in the law. They were too trusting. If the title was recorded in the courthouse, they assumed all was well. *Fee simple absolute.* Sounded like absolute ownership.

How little they knew.

People bought a piece of land in good faith and assumed

they owned it all the way down to magma. They assumed it has a *fee simple absolute* title.

But what most landowners don't realize is that, according to the law, surface land can be separated from the land underneath. You can own the top, but not the bottom. Or you can own the bottom, but not be entitled to any profit earned by mining for whatever was down there.

There were mineral rights and royalties and many other obscure kinds of rights—each of which can be sold separately, lost in divorce, and may or may not be remembered or recorded accurately with the title over the years.

That's what Gary was hunting for.

In his search through the various layers of documentation for this particular lot, he'd noticed a gap in the title. He kept digging.

An hour later, his left eye started to bother him, but he didn't stop. He was close. He blinked a few times to clear his vision. Another hour . . .

Two hours later, he looked up at the clock. 4:23. Just a few more minutes. He had a feeling . . .

It took two more trips and a visit to a private abstract office near the courthouse, but three days later, he struck gold.

He quickly perused the salient points of his find:

Mineral rights . . . 1858 . . . Mr. Martin J. Codweil . . . State of California . . . eight acres western coast, north of Devil's Claw, south of Bigsby Stream . . ."

Yep, it was all there.

And no one else knew about it.

Not the do-gooder building a sea otter center, not a naive young land developer building his dream, not the opportunistic investor, and definitely not the rapacious oil company wanting to suckle at Mother Nature's tit.

Only Gary had what they all needed.

Three of these players had the means to pay up. He was going to get those mineral rights and sell them to the highest bidder.

All he had to do now was find the descendants of one Mr. Martin J. Codweil and talk them into selling the mineral rights beneath several acres of prime California coastal real estate.

22

Since the public session of the city council meeting wouldn't start until 7:00 p.m., Ben would meet everyone at Logan's, walk down to Tava'e's, then drive them all to city hall in time to get good seats. Amy and Liam were going to try to snag three-minute speaking slots. Tava'e had insisted they stop by for a small meal before the meeting.

"Warriors don't go into battle on fast food," she sniffed when Logan said they were planning on grabbing something on the way.

Ben's work truck pull in around 4:00 p.m. He was showered, changed, and at her door in less than thirty minutes, knocking first, then letting himself in.

"You about ready?" Ben called up the stairs.

Logan was just getting out of the shower.

Towel drying her hair with one hand, grabbing her jeans off the bed with the other, she yelled down the stairs, "There's wine on the counter. I'll be right down!"

She wasn't speaking tonight, so her usual uniform of jeans and a T-shirt would be fine. Southern California had only two barely discernible seasons, so the only difference between her winter and summer wardrobes was changing boots to sandals.

By the time she got downstairs, Ben had the wine poured and on the coffee table. She joined him on the couch.

"Is Amy nervous about speaking tonight?" he asked.

"No, she's good. She's absolutely fearless when she's passionate about something," Logan said.

She took the glass Ben offered her and savored the aroma before taking a sip. Mmmm . . . 2010 Paso Robles cabernet. Even in the summer, a good red was a good red.

"What have you heard?" asked Logan. "You know a few of those guys on the council."

"Not much," Ben said. "Samson's okay. He's a Sierra Club guy from way back, and I think Vonagan is on Solange's side. Inglehart's been pretty vocal in the press. He's leading the charge for the local business owners and real estate people."

"What about Gable?"

"Don't know," Ben said, looking at his watch.

Logan looked at her phone: 4:55 and still no sign of Amy and Liam. Her daughter was many wonderful things, but prompt wasn't one of them. Just as she picked up her phone to call, they heard the crunch of gravel. They'd have to get a move on, but hopefully they'd still get to Tava'e's within an acceptable tardy range.

Ben corked the wine, and Logan lifted her jacket off the back of one of the bar stools. They met the kids on the walkway as Logan locked up.

"Hi, Ben! Hi, Mom!" Amy said, hugging each in turn as Liam locked up the rental car. "Sorry we're late!"

Amy's eyes sparkled with excitement. Long strawberry-blond

curls hugged her shoulders, lightly kissed by the sun. What a change from the pale, weak girl that stepped gingerly off the plane a few weeks ago from Africa. Amy radiated. Logan suspected being in love had something to do with her daughter's new glow, as well as working with Otter 1. It made her feel happy and sad, all at the same time.

"If we hustle, we'll still get there in time," Logan said.

"Yeah, I do *not* want to see Tava'e mad!" Amy said, eyes wide.

Navigating Killer Hill's narrow, buckled sidewalks took concentration, so conversation was limited until they got there.

When Liam opened the door, they were surprised to see the place was packed. Earnest and ebullient conversations swirled all around them. A delicious smell of roast meat made Logan salivate.

She didn't know everyone but recognized Solange Sauvage, Gina, and Dennis at one table and several people from Friends of the Sea Otter at another. They'd come by the center one morning to drop off some brochures. Tava'e, holding court from the back of the room, acknowledged their arrival with a wave and, once they were seated at what looked like the one remaining table, came over to administer crushing hugs.

"Talofa!"

"Wow!" Amy said, returning her hug, looking around. "It looks like everyone is here!"

Tava'e laughed. "Go get some food—eat first, talk later!"

She didn't have to tell them twice. Logan made a beeline for the buffet. The women in Logan's family, if not award-winning cooks, were definitely gold-medal eaters.

Three long tables were set up in front of the coffee counter, loaded with big bowls of coleslaw and fruit salads, platters of prosciutto-wrapped asparagus and rosemary baby pota-toes, and steaming trays of roast pork and chicken that made everyone realize how hungry they were. At the end of the spread was the biggest rice cooker Logan had ever seen—even in a Chinese restaurant—and, of course, Jean's contribution to the meal, fresh baguettes. Dominating a small, round table sat a sheet cake with "Otter 1" arched across the top in loopy script over a picture of the little pup's smiling whiskered face.

Tava'e's idea of a "small meal."

Epiphany was in charge of coffee and made sure everyone knew Danny made the cake. Later, he proudly manned the dessert table, carefully scooping either vanilla bean or choc-olate espresso ice cream to accompany generous servings of a dense, creamy, chocolate-ganache creation of his own design.

Blessed with the McKenna metabolism, Amy gleefully loaded up her plate at least as high as Ben's. Liam, it turned out, was the light eater of the group. He spent most of the time going over his notes.

A little after 6:00 p.m., as people were enjoying coffee and cake, Tava'e walked to the front of the room. She didn't need to get anyone's attention; her presence quietly commanded it.

"My friend would like to say a few words," she said.

A slight, self-possessed woman rose from her chair and faced the group. Minimal makeup and simple, neutral clothing drew your attention to an arresting face. Fierce black eyes shone out from softly creased skin framed by a cap of white hair.

Having worked with Solange on several of her sculpture projects, Ben knew her as well as anyone. Logan had only met the sculptress briefly. She never heard her say more than a few words. Gina was the daily presence at the center and the one quoted in the local paper.

In heavily accented English, Solange said, "First, I want to thank Tava'e for this beautiful and generous meal. It was delicious, and nourishing in so many ways. But even more, I want to thank her for supporting the foundation by providing a place for us to gather, talk, plan, and simply rest when we are tired. And of course, eat!" she added. She led a round of applause, which Tava'e acknowledged with a broad smile. "As many of you know, Tava'e does more for this community than any of us will ever realize."

Solange continued, "Tonight—*c'est très importante*! I know Gina will represent us well, as will those of you who will get to share your thoughts. But even if you can't speak, your presence at the meeting will send a message. A message that we value all life on this planet and are willing to fight for it.

"When I lost Mustafa, my husband, and, shortly after, my father, I thought my life was over. I returned home to find the sea otters, too, had gone. I accepted that as just another loss to bear. But otters are courageous adventurers. In spite of many efforts to keep them contained, a few brave ones managed to make it this far south. Every time one was spotted, it made me happy. But multiple barriers remained, and I had little hope they would ever return in numbers large enough to establish colonies here again.

"All of you, many organizations and individuals, give me hope and inspire me to do what I can. I am not a scientist or an environmental law expert. I sculpt. I do not have children, but if I did, I would want them to inherit a strong, healthy world—one with sea otters in it! I know you understand. I know I am, as you say, preaching to the choir."

Smiles and quiet laughter rippled around the room.

"I want to thank you—all of you. No matter what happens at this meeting tonight, or in the lawyers' offices tomorrow or in the coming months, I want you to know I will not give up. The center is essential and worth fighting for. We cannot do everything, but we can do this one thing."

23

Even with Solange's inspiring comments to fuel them, trudging back up Killer Hill was tougher than cruising down. Still, they were piled into Ben's car and on the road by six thirty. Traffic was light for a change, so they made it in time for the meeting, but just barely.

"I'll save you a seat," Logan said as she got out of the car and began walking in.

"OK—just make sure it's near a bathroom. I drank a gallon of coffee," Ben warned.

"Will do, big guy," Logan said.

Once inside, Logan, Amy, and Liam followed the other stragglers through the heavy double doors, searching for seats while Ben parked.

Someone opened a back door to create a cross breeze, which helped, but it was still stuffy with so many people crammed together. The fire code plaque on the wall set the seating capacity at 350. Looked like they were going to meet or exceed that limit by the time everyone was in.

Ben was in luck. A man seated in the last row of folding chairs, near the hall with the restrooms, got up to take a phone call. He and his wife gave their seats to Logan on their way out, before the meeting was called to order. Liam spotted two more seats up front. He sat down in one and put his notes down on the other, while Amy went to see if there were any speaking slots left.

"All full," Amy whispered to her mom a few minutes later, as she made her way past and up the crowded aisle.

Liam would be disappointed. He'd worked hard on his speech.

Logan leaned over to Ben, who had just joined her, handing him an agenda. "Gina's up first, then Scott, but not till the end of the meeting. I think they're hoping we all go home by then."

Council members were coming in from their closed session, taking their seats on the dais, so Ben just nodded and squeezed her hand.

All remaining seats were taken, with about a dozen people out in the overflow area. Logan couldn't help but notice how similar this room was to the school boardroom at the district office.

They must have been designed by the same architect. While the hoi polloi sat crowded together in the lowlands, the five council members were spaciously arranged around a curved, raised dais, topped with microphones arched to their mouths. The majority of the floor space was filled with two sections of folding chairs. *Padded* folding chairs, but still.

Legal counsel and assorted clerks and accountants sat at a side table, perpendicular to the dais, within easy reach should their services be required, while tonight's scheduled speakers sat below in the front row.

Gina's broad shoulders, height, and steel-gray curls made her easily identifiable. Dennis, still sporting the white bandage on the side of his head, sat on her right. He only came up to Gina's chin. Mutt and Jeff.

On the other side of a two-empty-seat, ersatz-Switzerland area sat the man Logan assumed was Scott Dekker.

Crisp. That was the overall impression. Dark hair neatly trimmed, clad for battle in a nice suit, shirt open at the collar. He sat still, looking straight ahead, elbows resting on his thighs. Laptop on the seat next to him. Ready.

When he turned his head a little to the left, Logan could see a prominent but not overly large nose, and delicate, rounded, seashell-shaped ears, just like Solange's. Her hair was white, while his was still dark, but the family resemblance was definitely there.

Not good.

Neither Solange nor Scott acknowledged the other's presence, although they must be acutely aware. Logan wondered if they had spoken in person yet or only through their attorneys.

The mayor, Carl Gable, took his place front and center and called the meeting to order. A former marine retired out of El Toro years ago, Carl owned both gas stations in Jasper, one on either end of town. When people got pissed off at one, they took their business to the other, not realizing he owned both. He always got a kick out of that.

While the mayor took care of opening business and the reading of the minutes from the last meeting, Logan surveyed the room. Rick had to work, but Paula was there. She sat a few rows up, with the Earthjustice people. The rest of Tava'e's dinner guests were scattered, most surrounding Solange protectively, who looked, but probably felt anything but, calm.

At seven forty, Carl introduced the first speaker.

"As most of you know, and from the minutes of our last meeting that were just read, the City of Jasper accepted the donation of lot 429 from Solange Sauvage over a year ago, and the planning commission, whose members are appointed by this council, approved the subsequent request to build the Southern Sea Otter Sanctuary and Education Center on that parcel of land."

He cleared his throat and continued.

"But as everyone who hasn't been a coma or on the space station in recent months knows, another party, Mr. Scott Dekker," he said, gesturing to Scott in the front row, "has since come forward and laid claim to lot 429. He has filed a request with the planning commission to build a residential development on this property."

Another pause.

He looked directly out to his audience. "This, ladies and gentlemen, is what we call a royal FUBAR."

Former military personnel in the audience grinned at the term.

"Fortunately, it's not a FUBAR we, the Jasper City Council, or the planning commission, will be responsible for fixing. We have been advised by counsel to let the court decide this matter before any further action is taken. In spite of the fact that no formal action can or will be taken by this council until the title dispute is resolved, we recognize the unusual circumstances and importance of this issue to our community.

"Since the two parties are representing issues critical to Jasper and its future, and in the interest of correcting the rumors that have been circulating"—at this he glowered at the audience—"the council has decided to let both sides speak their piece. And in the event Mr. Dekker is determined to be the rightful owner, the planning commission will again consider his request to build his development.

"You're all talking about it anyway—maybe someone will talk some sense tonight and this can be resolved between the two parties out of court, hopefully sometime before hell freezes over."

With this, he abruptly turned his focus to Gina. "Ms. Richards, you're up. You've got fifteen minutes."

Logan liked the way this guy started a meeting.

Gina rose and walked toward the front of the room. She took her place at the podium, which had been spirited into place while the mayor was speaking. She faced the audience and waited for them to finish shifting and achieve some level of comfort in their folding chairs.

Logan looked at Ben. She wasn't sure if going first was a good thing or not.

Gina adjusted the microphone and tapped it once to make sure it was working.

"Thank you to the mayor and all the members on the council. I appreciate this chance to speak with you today."

Gina's notes lay on the podium, but she didn't need them.

"I am not here to argue about who owns this land. I am here to speak about why this land, this very unique and rare piece of land, is critical to supporting the southern sea otter's return to this area, and why supporting the southern sea otter's return is critical to us—to each and every person here.

"Why do we need to save the sea otter? What does it matter if this furry mammal, cute as it is, which once numbered in the millions, is now down to a few thousand individual animals, clustered mostly in the Bay Area? Why do we need this Southern Sea Otter Sanctuary and Education Center? And why here?

"Simply put, we need the sea otter. We need healthy oceans, and rebuilding the southern sea otter population is vital. Until recently, the ocean—the ecosystem right outside our door—was assumed to be immune to human activity, immense enough to absorb anything we dumped into it and so full of resources, it could never be depleted. We know better now.

"Oceans are the lifeblood of our species—of all life on Earth. To heal this essential ecosystem, we need to clean up our messes and help bring it back into balance. Even though seventy-five percent of ocean species have already gone extinct due to overharvesting, pollution, and a myriad of other human factors, it is not hopeless or beyond fixing. There is a lot we can do to restore biodiversity to this important ecosystem."

Gina nodded to Dennis, who waved and held up a handout from a stack in a roller cart at his feet.

"I won't take your time now, but after the meeting, please take one of the handouts, which provides specific environmental success stories, where people have worked together to solve these problems where they live: coral reefs recovered, wildlife returned, and, right here at home, thanks to Nancy Caruso's Get Inspired! and many of you, vital kelp beds restored right off our shores."

Here she nodded at Tava'e's relatives, who applauded loudly.

"Damage can be reversed. But we need to start right here, right now. Since we're all dependent on the oceans, we all need to do our part.

"Okay, so much for the background. If you're interested in the science behind all this, I'll be happy to recommend websites and books that will explain it in more detail. That brings us back to why we need the center. To help a habitat or ecosystem rebound, we focus on the keystone species. The southern sea otter, a predator, is a keystone species. Protect and bring the otters back, and the whole ecosystem rebounds. All species in an ecosystem, or habitat, rely on each other.

"When we got rid of otters, it wiped out the kelp beds. Sea

otters feed on sea urchins, controlling their population. When sea otters disappeared from overhunting off our coasts, uncontrolled sea-urchin populations ate the habitat's kelp. Kelp, or giant seaweed, is a major source of food and shelter for the ecosystem. Some species of crabs, snails, and even migrating geese depend on kelp for food. Many types of fish use the huge kelp forests to hide from predators. Without sea otters to control the urchin population, the entire ecosystem collapsed.

"I know my time is almost gone, so I'll wrap this up. In order for humans to thrive, we need to heal the damage we have done, particularly in our fragile coastal waters, and help restore the natural balance. And that requires biodiversity. That requires the return of the southern sea otter.

"Efforts at transplanting sea otters and plunking them down in new environments, trying to establish new colonies artificially, such as the attempt off San Nicolas, have not worked. For those interested, a more detailed list of reasons for this can be found in the materials available to you as you leave.

"Just know that even with the best care and nutrient-rich environment, it's tough for a baby sea otter to survive long enough to have and nurture offspring. Only twenty-five percent of sea otters make it to adulthood. It takes another three or four years before they are capable of breeding. If we're lucky enough to raise a wild sea otter from newborn to successful, independent, breeding adult in a marine rescue facility, its chances of survival upon release into the wild are even slimmer. They can be chewed up by boats, poisoned by cat litter pollution or fertilizer waste that flows to the sea through storm drains, or, more and more frequently, mistaken for a seal, chomped on, and spit out by a shark, like Otter 1's mom was. She didn't survive. It's a miracle her pup did.

"And what about the three thousand otters clustered in the Bay Area? Surely they will keep the species going. The raw truth is, the entire colony could be wiped out in one oil spill. We need more otter colonies in more coastal areas in order to up the chances that this keystone species will survive. Which brings me to the whole point of my standing up here talking your ears off: the Sea Otter Sanctuary and Education Center."

More cheers from the supporters.

Gina opened her laptop and signaled to someone in the back of the room to turn down the lights. She put up a slideshow that took her audience on a tour of the facilities, explaining the role of each room and how it would provide aid for marine-mammal rescue, injured otters, and oil-spill recovery and showing a fully equipped research lab, in addition to tanks and trainers for rehabilitating rescued, orphaned otter pups. She ended with an animation of otters frolicking in the aquarium on the main floor, in front of a throng of enthralled school children.

Nice touch.

"Finally," she said as Dennis turned the lights back on, "everyone in this room knows that available coastal property is not just rare in Southern California—it's almost nonexistent. The piece of land Solange Sauvage generously donated is not only uniquely situated for this center, but we are located in a prime habitat for an otter colony to establish itself. It's the only land available for it anywhere near here. That said, I have an announcement to make.

"Thanks to so many individuals and environmental groups working together, the Southern Sea Otter Sanctuary and Education Center has not only been built, but, as of a few hours ago, has cleared the last certification hurdle and been successfully approved . . ."

Thunderous applause broke out among the center's supporters in the audience, and several of the board members smiled broadly.

When they quieted down, Gina continued, ". . . has been successfully approved by the Fish and Wildlife Service to provide sea mammal rescue and medical services, orphaned pup rehabilitation, and educational programs. We will open as scheduled August 28!"

Gina waited for the enthusiastic applause to die down before closing her remarks.

"The otters are trying to return. We can't force this process, but as otters migrate down in ones and twos, we can support them. We need to be there for them. Let's start with this little girl," Gina said, taping an eight-by-ten color photo of Otter 1 on the front of the podium, facing the audience. "Let's save *her*."

A final burst of applause rang out, and several people rose to their feet.

Gina gathered her papers, which she had barely referred to, and returned to her seat. Carl banged his gavel to quiet the crowd.

"Scott Dekker, you have the floor. Your allotted time is the same."

24

Everyone quieted down.

Logan wondered what Dekker could possibly say that would change anyone's mind after Gina's thorough, intelligent presentation. She'd covered all the bases, answered all the questions. Who could argue with anything she'd said?

Hesitant at first, and not without a few boos from Tava'e's group, which were quickly silenced by one look from the mayor, Scott quietly removed the picture of Otter 1 Gina had taped to the front of the podium and placed it upside down on the table next to the podium.

He cleared his throat, straightened his papers, and looked up at the crowd.

"Good evening. My name is Scott Dekker, and I appreciate the opportunity to share the facts with you—*all* the facts. I don't have a fancy slide show. I don't have a wealthy benefactor. All I have is my land. Yes, *my* land."

He unfolded a thin blue piece of paper and held it up.

Everyone could see the even, angular handwriting of a personal letter, signed at the bottom.

"This letter, recently authenticated by handwriting expert Ms. Granley Bishop, was written by Robert Sauvage, my biological father. It clearly states in no uncertain terms that he gives me, without encumbrance, this specific piece of land, lot 429."

He looked out at his audience.

"The letter is to my mother, so I will not read it in full here, but even Ms. Sauvage's attorney agrees it is authentic."

Everyone looked at Solange, whose face betrayed nothing. She remained ramrod straight, collected, hands in her lap.

Logan was stunned.

Is this new information? Does that mean the center is lost? What about Solange's deed? She had been given the property by the probate court when her father died. She built the center in good faith. How could this ever be straightened out fairly?

"While, as the mayor said, this title dispute will be resolved officially by the court, I have every confidence my rights will be upheld. But that still leaves the question for the planning commission, some of whom I see here tonight, and for the members of this community, about the best way to use that land. Tonight, I am here to set the record straight.

"First. The otters are never coming back. This area will not support them. Whether we like it or not, the world has changed. Any injured sea otters can be patched up at the aquarium in Long Beach and sent up north to Monterey for rehabilitation. People came, people hunted. People are here. Otters aren't. So instead of trying to turn back the clock to some mythical, pristine time, we need to deal with reality."

Scott braced for another round of boos, but although anger emanated from much of the audience, they kept quiet, allowing him to continue.

"But I'm not here to talk about sea otters. I'm also not here to build a mini mall, halfway house, or low-rent apartment complex. I'm not even here to build another cookie-cutter subdivision. Jasper is unique and beautiful. I remember coming here as a child—my mom brought me down here—the natural beauty, the ocean, the hills. There isn't another community like it anywhere. Far from being the big, bad land developer out to destroy the unique character of this place, I'm the guy whose project will enhance it and help it continue. I believe responsible growth is possible, without changing what's great about Jasper."

At this point, a few more faces in the crowd looked interested.

"And Jasper needs help. I've done a little research, and this community is hurting. For years, the liberal elite have kept this community from growing its economic base. God forbid you should build a decent-size grocery store, let alone a gas station. During the recession, while the rest of us were losing our shirts, wealthy citizens in Jasper, and all across this country, blocked every possible income-producing business or development they could. 'No growth,' they call it here. Just so some of these guys"—here he gestured vaguely to the left of the room, which contained Gina and Solange—"could stroll along their private beaches undisturbed. They didn't care about us, the little guys. They had theirs. It was okay for them to own the big house or the hotel or restaurant in town, but God forbid anyone else try to lift themselves up through hard work and build something for themselves. Those efforts were blocked, every time."

Several heads in the audience nodded in agreement, and there was an uncomfortable shuffling of feet.

"My proposed community, Pacific Shores, will not only be spectacularly beautiful, designed to blend into its natural surroundings, but will bring in much-needed tax revenue.

And for those genuinely concerned about the environment, the entire project utilizes passive solar design. Recycled water will be used exclusively for all external property needs.

"And notice I said genuine environmentalists. With all due respect to her scientific credentials, the former speaker is employed by Solange Sauvage, whose only basis for building this aquarium is her emotional attachment to some animals from her childhood that no longer naturally exist here.

"This project will also provide jobs. As far as I can tell, Ms. Sauvage has never worked for a living like you and I. Supported by our father and his wealthy friends. Not exactly in touch with the middle class."

Scott's face hardened somewhat, and he spoke the next few words carefully. "I, on the other hand, like most of you here tonight, *do* work for a living. Have always worked. During the years that Ms. Sauvage was off in Paris, sipping wine in cafés, I was working my way through college, hammering nails and laying pipe."

Logan looked over at Solange. Her head moved back slightly at these last comments, as if she'd been physically hit with his words.

"Even when I was losing everything during the recession, I honored my contracts. I paid my bills. Now all I want is what's rightfully mine. I deserve my fair shot. I've earned it," he said, looking directly at Solange.

Straightening the papers, Scott concluded his remarks. "Jasper will benefit a whole lot more from Pacific Shores than it will by being turned into a dilettante's project: a million-dollar first-aid station for the one or two otters who wander down the coast every couple of years.

"I ask each of you to go to PacificShoresJasper.com to take a look at the development for yourselves. See how it will benefit this community and how it will help you if you are a small-business owner in town. There is also a contact page. Feel free to e-mail me with any questions or concerns." He smiled apologetically out at his audience. "It may take a while, because I don't have a secretary, but I promise to answer each e-mail myself.

"And one more thing for everyone who lives in Jasper to consider. Due to misplaced sympathies, Jasper has seen an increase in the homeless population and in halfway houses, resulting in more incidents of crime and vandalism.

"Pacific Shores, which includes world-class security, would reduce crime while increasing property values. Rising tides lift all boats. I'll bet every homeowner in this room would welcome seeing some appreciation. Home values have been flat in this area for years.

"Go to the website. You'll see that approving Pacific Shores is not only the right thing to do, it's right for Jasper. Thank you."

Scott's speech was met mostly with silence as he took his seat, but there was a scattering of applause and quite a few thoughtful faces, including several on the council.

Although she was still strongly in Solange's camp, Logan felt Scott made some good points. His arguments would not be easy to ignore.

25

1963

The faded, green Volkswagen, packed and running, driver's door open, sat waiting. Gangly eighteen-year-old Gary Schofield was off to college. Father and son stood awkwardly together in the driveway.

Giving him a clumsy pat on the shoulder, Dad stood back so Gary could fold himself into the car.

"You'll do great, Son," he said.

Gary got in.

"Just finish school. A four-year degree will put bread on the table," he said.

Gary nodded and drove away.

For a while, his father watched him go.

Odd duck, that boy.

If he hadn't driven his wife to the hospital himself, he'd have sworn the child wasn't a Schofield. Shaking off the millisecond of reflection, he turned to walk back inside. It was Wednesday, meatloaf night.

○ ○ ○ ○ ○

When Gary got to Berkeley, most courses were already closed. He wound up filling his schedule with odd selections, just to fulfill his undergrad requirements: Greek and Roman Mythology and a course entitled Language, Truth, and Logic.

In the logic class, he quickly learned he had a gift for absorbing large amounts of information, spitting them back for the test, but also forming *from* that vast amount of knowledge cohesive, cogent arguments.

It was stimulating. Formal or informal, he always won the debates. Business school was impacted anyway, so he landed in classics, receiving his baccalaureate in rhetoric four years later.

When it became clear that all the McDonald's jobs were taken by former classics graduates, Gary enrolled in law school. Not only was he going to put bread on the table, but next to the bread would be some very fine wine. He didn't care about putting a roof over anyone's head. He had no intention of ever marrying and definitely didn't want any children.

During law school, and the subsequent punishing workload at his first and only law firm, Gary thrived. He had no trouble with long hours. He'd never needed more than four hours of sleep per night, and he had no personal life.

But after three years, he'd had enough. He was a good lawyer, but not the best. In college, he'd been a big fish in a little pond. Here, all the fish were big. When it was obvious he'd never make partner, he struck out on his own. Hired an answering service and a virtual office. Brought on adjunct help as needed. He focused on corporate law and contracts. Family or criminal law did not appeal to him. People were idiots. He wanted to deal with people as little as possible.

DEVIL'S CLAW

SATURDAY, JULY 4

Gary tossed his briefcase onto the front passenger seat as he got into his two-year-old Lincoln. Black. Leather interior. Like clockwork, he traded them in every two years. Always a year old, never a new one. He let someone else take that initial depreciation hit. The Lincoln accommodated his six-foot-five frame.

Preparing to back out, he checked the rearview mirror. Mournful eyes looked back at him. The dark circles he'd developed in law school had grown into droopy bags. There was surgery, he knew, but it wasn't top on his to-do list. Besides, in his business, looking tired was an asset. Clients thought you worked harder for them.

He reached up and straightened the mirror, thinking about the meeting. Scott wasn't happy but hadn't taken the news too badly. Felix was playing it cool. Felix held all the cards. At least he thought he did.

Gary smirked.

Putting on some sunglasses, he exited the parking lot and got on the freeway. Another parking lot, but he didn't mind. It gave him time to reflect and savor the details of last week's trip. The visit to Marshall, Arkansas, had been quite successful.

It being a warm, humid night when he arrived, the couple he'd come to see walked him back to a screened-in porch, which overlooked their small farm. They were short and doughy—like little dumplings.

The wife prepared a coffee tray and cookies.

"Did you know there's a town named Jasper just up the road? Newton County, right honey, or is it Pope?" the woman asked her husband.

She turned back to Gary.

"We're in Pope," she informed him.

As if he cared.

The woman's drawn-out drawl made Gary want to slap her, or better yet, choke the life out of her. Still, he made small talk with the two dumplings as best he could for a while, before getting to the point. No need to rush.

At first, the morons didn't understand.

"You mean, we own some land that is about to fall into the ocean, and you want to buy it from us?" the woman said. Apparently, Mrs. Dumpling did all the talking for the pair. Mr. Dumpling limited his input to grunts and wondering if it was going to rain.

Gary kept it simple and lied. He did not bother to clarify the difference between mineral rights and surface land, so he said yes, she'd inherited some land when her father, Martin, died. They didn't know about it because it had never been recorded.

"Your father may not even have known he owned it, as it may have been left to him by his father or grandfather," Gary explained.

They looked at him blankly. He'd have to wrap this up fast.

He continued. "It's on a very narrow lot, recently condemned, deemed unstable due to landslides."

Again, he didn't bother to explain the difference between landownership and mineral rights. He was hoping they wouldn't ask.

Which brought Gary to the reason he was here, sitting with them on their back porch.

He only wanted to buy their land, he said, because he had property just behind it, safe for now on a granite slab, and hoped some sliver of the lot in front would remain after the largest chunk slid into the ocean, which could happen at any time. Simply put, he wanted a buffer between him and the Pacific Ocean. It was an El Niño year, and heavy rain was expected.

The couple had never been to California but knew all about the unstable San Andreas Fault, they'd seen the movie. They also knew about the even more unstable people who chose to live there.

Gary raised his cup to his lips and pretended to take another drink of his now tepid coffee. Maybe a little nudge was needed.

Oh, and by the way, his grandmother had been from Arkansas, he told them. No, he didn't know the name of her town. Miller was her name. Fine people. She was from somewhere vaguely east in the state—the opposite corner of this little farm.

When he got to the part about his being willing to buy the land from them for a couple hundred thousand dollars, the woman's eyes widened, and her penciled eyebrows lifted.

Mrs. Dumpling kept her cool and kicked her husband under the table to keep him from ruining everything. She hadn't just fallen off the turnip truck. Wouldn't pay to show too much excitement. Something didn't smell right with this guy, but what did she care? As long as his check was good, she didn't care why he really wanted to buy her land. Two hundred thousand dollars would go a long way in Arkansas.

Buying a few minutes to think while her mind buzzed with enthusiasm, she said, "More coffee, Mr. Schofield?"

Imagine being willing to pay two hundred thousand dollars for a worthless piece of property that was going to fall into the ocean any day. But she knew it was probably nothing to him. Her cousin Franny moved to Sacramento, California, married a California man. They paid over $450,000 for a tiny box of a house that wouldn't sell for $150,000 here. They just didn't seem to understand the value of a hard-earned dollar out there. But she did.

As the man droned on about his relatives up north, she allowed herself a sliver of excitement. They could pay off the farm. Maybe even go see her sister in Atlanta. They could go to Hawaii!

They kept the conversation going until they'd run out of relatives to talk about.

Patience up, Gary produced the papers for them to sign.

He watched as their dimpled fingers moved the pen across the pages, signing and initialing in all the designated places.

Both parties satisfied, he handed them the cashier's check and placed the documents in his briefcase.

It was late, but he had no intention of spending the night anywhere in the state.

I've probably lost twenty IQ points already.

By the time he got to the airport, he'd already decided which of the interested parties—Solange, Felix, or Bill—he was going to approach first, now that he had the mineral rights free and clear.

By the time he landed at John Wayne, he had the features and accessories picked out for his next Lincoln. He even entertained the luxury of buying a new one.

26

An efficient young woman sporting a boxy blue medical smock and supportive shoes pushed open the door next to the reception desk. Clipboard in hand, holding the door open with her hip, she scanned the waiting room.

"Mr. Schofield?"

Gary rose from his chair. Ducking through, he followed her into a warren of passageways and regularly spaced, closed doors.

Manila file tucked under her arm, she walked him all the way back, keeping up a stream of chatter along the way.

Yes, he was fine. No, he wasn't here to see the doctor about anything. He was just here to get the results of his tests.

They stopped briefly at the scale near the nurse's station to weigh in. She noted the specifics on his chart—he'd lost a few pounds—then took her charge the rest of the way down the hall. Placing his folder in the clear plastic holder outside room eight, she instructed him to go in and take a seat, the doctor would be right with him.

Right.

Doctors, as Gary was beginning to find out, were never "right with you." At least he was done with all the tests. Why the doctor ordered so many, he didn't know, but probably it was to protect themselves from litigation—from lawyers like him. The irony was not lost on Gary.

Hopefully, today's visit was just to get whatever medicine he needed or schedule whatever procedure would fix this problem.

He knew he'd overworked his eyes, and the left one was giving him fits. It started with a splitting headache that just wouldn't let up. Next, he started seeing spots, and it just refused to focus. He'd been wearing a patch on the thing for a week now. Hopefully it was rested, and they'd give him some drops or something and send him on his way.

He had work to do.

That's the only reason he was here. Get this thing fixed. Get back to work.

Twenty minutes later, Dr. Te knocked lightly and walked in.

About damn time . . . Why do they knock? What do they think we're doing in here? Playing with ourselves?

"Hello, Gary," the doctor said. "How's the eye doing today?"

"You tell me. I've kept the patch on," Gary said. "What do I need to do now?"

Just give me the damn medicine and let me get out of here.

"Well, that's what I wanted to talk with you about. Before I give you all of the test results, I want you to understand you have options. I've gone over everything several times, and I'm afraid the news is not good . . ."

As Gary waited, confused, Dr. Te continued.

". . . glioblastoma . . . stage four . . . inoperable brain cancer . . ."

"What?" Gary cleared his throat, which was suddenly very dry. He hadn't heard much after the "C word."

Dr. Te, having seen this before, was prepared. He handed his newly diagnosed cancer patient a bottle of water and repeated what he'd just said.

After a longer explanation of his findings, Gary seemed to accept, if not fully absorb, the news that he had inoperable cancer. Brain cancer.

"What does this mean, exactly? How long can I expect to live . . . normally? Independently?" he asked.

Dr. Te cleared his throat. "Of course, there are always exceptions, some patients live up to five more years, but on average, with aggressive treatment, about fourteen months. Although at this stage, the best you can do is try to shrink the tumor, slow the progress, and manage your symptoms."

Having delivered this news many times before, Dr. Te gave his patient some more time for this information to sink in. Everyone reacted differently. Dr. Te wondered how he would react if someone delivered the news to him.

"Do you have someone? Is there anyone you'd like me to call?" he asked, finally breaking the silence.

"No."

Gary's one good eye stared at the art on the wall. A lovely beach scene.

Dr. Te took a more professional, wrap-this-conversation-up tone. "You can probably expect to continue as you have been for a few more months, but you could experience more severe symptoms at any time—as early as the next few weeks. They will be intermittent. Not a smooth progression—more of a zigzag. Due to the particular area of the brain your tumor is in, these symptoms may be visual, emotional, or behavioral and gaps in memory." He placed a brochure in Gary's hands.

"These can be frightening when they occur. This is not something you want to deal with alone. I strongly recommend that you educate yourself as best you can and contact one of these support groups."

Dr. Te was already rising from his stool, shedding his avuncular role.

Gary, who was eye to eye with his doctor, even sitting down, only half listened to Dr. Te's instructions to stop at the receptionist's station on the way out to schedule another appointment for the end of the week, to begin chemo and radiation treatments. He absently took the brochure and endured the doctor's firm handshake.

Somehow he managed to find the exit and make it out to his car.

He did not stop to make another appointment for Friday.

27

Gary wasn't giving up. Dr. Te offered nothing but an arsenal of prescriptions, radiation, and chemotherapy, ending with a one-way trip to the hospital. Not much hope there. But there were doctors, even in the States, who said they had options. Just not options approved by the FDA or the AMA.

He found one. A woman doctor out in Oakland. Only accepted cash. Made him sign some kind of "I'm doing this of my own free will" pledge and a bunch of papers swearing not to divulge the secrets of "the Treatment." All legal CYA, nothing that phased Gary.

He told no one about his diagnosis but took a few days off until the medications his regular doctor gave him minimized his symptoms. Western medicine was good for something. Begged off any meetings he didn't need to attend. Claimed the flu. Gave his eyes a rest whenever he could.

His first appointment with Dr. Conklin at the New Hope Cancer Center was in five minutes.

Her office told him to block out three hours. He hoped he didn't have to do any chanting and that candles and a lot of touching were not involved.

Things did not go well.

The Treatment? The one he'd paid three thousand dollars for (and that was just phase one)? Phase one of the Treatment consisted of spending the first hour filling out page after page of medical history, which he'd expected, and a very personal questionnaire, which he had not, including his sexual habits. He left those blank.

The next phase was detox, which consisted of sticking your feet in a tub of water for half an hour. Rusty-orange, scummy foam gathered on the surface, dutifully exclaimed over and scraped off when the timer went off by an overly enthusiastic medical assistant of some type. At the same time, another medical assistant, or maybe she was a nurse, conducted something called chelation therapy. She stuck a needle in his arm, hooked him up to an IV bag, and set another timer. Something going in, something coming out. Looked like blood. Gary looked away. Chelation was supposed to get rid of any heavy metals he might have hanging around in his system, feeding the cancer.

"Heavy metals have been shown to contribute to many negative health issues, including less-obvious ones, like anger," she added, pointedly. "Chelation therapy dissipates all kinds of emotional baggage we carry around unnecessarily."

This mega fun was followed by an infrared sauna and massage, which he firmly declined, much to the disapproval of the massage therapist.

"But, Mr. Schofield, this is the best part! We just stirred everything up—we need to flush out your lymph nodes," she informed him. "We need to get the whole team in there fighting that cancer!"

He assumed she was pushing because she would not be paid if he turned down the massage. He certainly wasn't going to pay her. Or tip her—if that's what one did in these places.

The pièce de résistance was a meeting with his personal life and nutrition coach. At least she had a diploma on the wall declaring her to be an actual nutritionist. After prescribing a cleansing diet of sprouts, raw cruciferous vegetables, and wheatgrass shots, she got to the life-coaching part.

This is where she lost him. When she suggested he avail himself of the $250-an-hour anger elimination course at the center, not included in the initial $3,000 fee he'd already paid, he flipped her clipboard into the trash and walked out.

Apparently the chelation hadn't dissipated enough of his negative emotions.

THURSDAY, JULY 23

Dr. Te called.

Gary listened.

Since he was refusing anything but pain medication, no treatment at all—no radiation, no chemotherapy—and had refused to schedule further appointments, the doctor had no choice, his words, but to deliver the news that Gary was looking at months versus years.

He could not emphasize enough how dangerous it was for Gary, and others, if he continued to drive, continued to refuse treatment . . . blah, blah, blah.

And just to make sure Gary had a very clear picture, he plainly laid out the stark future without treatment. There would be blackouts, sudden mood swings, extreme pain, mental confusion, and, eventually, death, uncushioned by medical palliatives.

Is this what Gary wanted?

Well, no.

But Gary hadn't yet exhausted all possibilities.

He had one more option.

Between dodging meetings with Felix, Gary had been busy. What was it someone had said? *The absence of alternatives clears the mind marvelously.*

Einstein? Emerson? Didn't matter.

Now that he might not have the luxury, Gary discovered he deeply wanted to live. Preferably someplace warm, sitting under a palm tree with a beautiful woman bringing him Glenlivet 18 on the rocks. Whatever life he had left, he decided it would not be spent sitting in beige rooms or staring at a computer screen, sifting through the detritus of other people's lives. He pictured all the legal documents he'd generated over his career, placed end to end in an infinite loop—a kind of equatorial paper belt.

What a waste.

Mexico had beautiful women. And palm trees. And, he discovered, cancer clinics.

He'd done his homework. Researched. Sure, it was pie in the sky, but these places, even if they didn't deliver on saving his life, had strong drugs not allowed in the US and were located on long, sandy beaches in luxury accommodations, where he could live—really live—for whatever time he had left.

In general, living in Mexico was cheap, but the clinics weren't. Not the luxury residential ones he was looking at. And why settle for less?

All he needed was a little more cash . . . And he knew just where to get it.

The next twenty-four hours were busy ones. Operating on autopilot, Gary got to work. Picked a clinic. Travelers checks. Cash. Reservations out of John Wayne. Two days from now, he'd be in Mexico—that would give him plenty of time to do what he needed to do.

He'd have to leave the Lincoln in the States. Regretful, but necessary. He couldn't picture a Lincoln in Mexico anyway.

Guadalajara. The clinic he chose specialized in brain cancers like his. Oasis de Milagro Clinic was a pricey, one-shot deal. They either cured you in a month or two, or you died. He appreciated the honesty. And the fact that no one there asked about his anger issues.

28

He sat at the kitchen bar for another minute, mentally reviewing his to-do list, looking out the plain, square window of his minuscule kitchen to the off-white stucco wall opposite. Beige trim. Like every other townhouse within a thousand miles of here.

Beige. Like the rest of his life.

What was he forgetting? He didn't used to need to write anything down. He couldn't trust his brain anymore. Lately, he sometimes had to strain to remember even simple things, like whether he'd brushed his teeth or put gas in the car.

Pressing on his left eye to alleviate the omnipresent tingling and twitching, which he knew presaged stabbing pain, Gary climbed the narrow staircase to his bedroom. He rolled his suitcase out of the closet and lifted it onto the bed. He began to fill it with his usual travel kit: two suits, three dress shirts, Ferragamos, belt . . .

Stopping mid toss, he let a recently laundered (medium

starch) dress shirt slip out of his hand to the floor and laughed.

Won't be needing dress shirts in Mexico!

Feeling better already, leaving the mostly empty suitcase on the bed, he trotted back downstairs. He'd just buy what he needed when he got there. Maybe he'd get some shorts or those loose linen pants plantation owners in the tropics favored. Go commando. Probably not.

Back in the dining room, he scanned the contents of his briefcase. Everything seemed to be in place. Passport. Mineral rights paperwork. An extra copy tucked away in a safety deposit box. Laptop. Chargers. Everything was there.

He clicked it shut and took a last look around the place.

Keys in one hand, briefcase in the other, he locked the front door and walked to his car. Three minutes later, he pointed his car toward Southern California.

In several hours, the freeway exit said Castaic. Castaic? What the hell did that mean?

The blinding pain was coming, but he'd learned to keep it at bay for a while with deep, even breaths. Soon, he'd have to pull over at a rest stop for a few hours' rest. Real sleep was something more than he could hope for.

Getting through LA would take at least two hours, no matter what time of day he got there. No way to avoid that, but he'd still get into Jasper by late afternoon.

He'd already called and set up the meet.

It took three stopovers and the last of his pain pills, but he finally made it. If only the pain would stop. He arrived at the sea otter center just as a tired sun hovered above the horizon.

He pulled straight into the side entrance as directed and parked next to an older model, small silver Audi he assumed belonged to Ms. Sauvage. The upper lot was empty.

He glanced at his watch. Relieved. Just enough time to

conduct his business and make his flight. It was scheduled to depart SNA at 10:07 p.m. Red-eye to Guadalajara. He'd pump himself full of alcohol and sleep the whole way.

Patting his briefcase for reassurance, Gary turned off the engine and got out of the car. He reached into the back seat to retrieve another item, a North Face rolling bag, which was empty.

Solange Sauvage, expressionless, stood silently waiting for him, silhouetted in the doorway. Green light from the exit sign mingled with the light flowing through the blue glass on each side of the door, transforming her into a diminutive, female Poseidon.

A stiff breeze sharply snapped the metal grommets of the canvas banners against the metal flagpoles above, startling the seagulls perched there.

Shutting the door behind him after he ducked in, Solange lead her guest back, past an office and into a large lab.

Gary looked around the room and down the hall.

"Don't worry, no one's here. The volunteers won't come in until tomorrow morning, and I sent Gina and Dennis down to La Jolla to evaluate an injured sea otter. They'll be gone overnight. I offered to take their shift."

Solange walked around the island and took a seat on one of the swivel stools, facing him, delicate hands folded on the cool, empty surface.

Her black eyes glittered with unidentifiable emotion. She indicated he should take one of the stools on his side. The sun's last rays streamed in the back doors, flooding the gleaming surface of the lab table with a brief but fiery lava red.

Gary walked over but remained standing. Rolling the proffered seat out of the way with his foot, he placed his briefcase on the slab, popped open the locks, and lifted the top, removing the mineral rights deed for lot 429. Pushed it across where she could read it.

"It's all there. Registered and filed, rightfully mine."

Solange glanced at the papers but did not reach for them or respond.

Gary continued, feeling a little nervous. This wasn't going as smoothly as he'd anticipated. Something was definitely wrong.

"It's worth a lot more than a million," he continued. "You're getting a bargain. Lucky for you, a million is all I need." He didn't see a duffel bag or briefcase anywhere. "Where's the money?"

Solange continued to gaze at him steadily, but said nothing.

Finally, she cleared her throat and looked him right in the eye. "I don't have it," she said simply.

He was momentarily stunned. What came out of Gary's mouth was more sputter than anything else, and he took half a step back, as if he'd been physically struck. He definitely had not been expecting this.

What did she mean she didn't have it? Of course she had it. She had no choice! If she wanted to save her precious sea otters, she'd jump at the chance to secure the mineral rights so no one could drill for oil under her little aquarium.

This was supposed to be easy, a quick stop on the way to the airport.

"Give me the money!" he raised his voice.

Solange stayed where she was.

"You have to pay!" he said, leaning forward, then starting to walk around the five square feet of lab table separating them.

This is ridiculous! Is she going to make me beat it out of her?

"You're being filmed, Mr. Schofield," Solange informed him calmly.

"What?!" Gary said, wildly looking around the room.

"Oh, you won't see them. The cameras are hidden. I had the security system beefed up after Dennis was attacked. From your arrival to your latest vile threat, every slimy word has been recorded." She let this sink in, then continued. "I'm not giving you any money—not one dime. You can't just extort money from people," she said, her voice rising in quiet determination. "You can't just demand payment—this isn't some mob movie." Solange stood. "I think it's time for you to leave," she said.

The room was almost dark. In silhouette, she looked like a delicate, snowy egret, guarding her nest from an overbearing hawk, just inches away now.

"You lose, Mr. Schofield. Go ahead and sell the mineral rights. No one is going to let anyone drill for oil under a sea otter sanctuary. That paper is worthless!"

With that, Solange reached for a button hidden under the counter.

All reason fled what was left of Gary's working brain.

29

Fury and frustration rose in equal measure. Almost of its own accord, his left arm shot out and grabbed and yanked her toward him. Long, sinewy fingers wrapped tightly around her throat, he effortlessly lifted her completely off the ground.

Solange writhed and fought, scratching desperately at his hands. Eyes bulged, face contorted with the effort. Gary looked on dispassionately, as if someone else were doing the strangling. Finally, Solange's body went limp. He let her slip silently from his fingers into a small heap on the tiled floor.

The killing brought an unexpected calm. For no particular reason, Gary went through her purse and was rewarded with eighty dollars in twenties. Must have just been to the ATM. Let them film him. He'd just murdered a woman. He didn't think adding petty theft would be any big deal. Besides, she was probably bluffing about the security cameras. Like those fake "ABC Security Service" or the "Beware of Attack Dog" signs people stuck in their lawns or in the corner of their windows. Useless.

He put the file back in his briefcase. It was still valuable—just to someone else. He had two other buyers—and they didn't care about disturbing sea otters.

Gary's only job now was to get to the airport and make his flight. He needed to get out of the country as soon as possible. It was dark now, but he didn't turn on any lights. He could see well enough. Didn't need to have some beach jogger identifying him.

Solange hadn't made it to the panic button, but he didn't know how often the security company checked their video feed, if there really was one. The panic button could have been a dummy, too. No sense taking chances.

Felix or Bill would come up with the cash. He could handle everything from Mexico. Should have started with the two obvious sources, anyway. He should have known anyone idealistic enough to throw their money away by building a home away from home for sea otters wouldn't think practically and just pay the money.

Stupid woman.

Before he could leave the lab, he heard a heavy clunk. Something mechanical, like a gear, engaged across the room.

Now what?

The elevator.

No time to hide the body.

He quickly crouched down behind the center island.

"Gina? Dennis? Anybody home?"

Gary risked a quick look around the side. In the dark, he could see his visitor was a kid, but since his eyes were adjusting to the dark, the kid couldn't see him.

Carrying a large, unwieldy stack of clothes, pushing his feet ahead to avoid stumbling, the boy was edging his way toward the cubbies along the right wall.

Gary held his breath, waiting. Maybe the kid wouldn't notice the dead body on the floor. He wasn't sure he could see it from that angle.

"Somebody want to turn a light on in here?" the boy called.

No, someone doesn't.

The boy was Jeff, and the laundry he carried was a gift of love.

All the volunteers got two T-shirts, a pair of overalls, and boots. The boots got hosed off and stored in the bottom cubby at the end of each shift. Purses, keys, and any clothing you didn't want to wind up smelling like fish was stored on the top shelf. The rain ponchos and welders masks hung from hooks next to the cubbies. Everyone had to wear one when working with the otter.

Since laundry facilities didn't come with Amy's summer cottage rental, Jeff volunteered to do her otter duds with his.

"My mom doesn't mind at all," he'd insisted, "she won't let me wash my fishy clothes with anything else, anyway—might as well throw yours in there, too," he told her when Amy said he didn't have to do that. It was as close as he was likely to get to Amy, he knew. He'd seen her fiancé. Tall, handsome, smart. Had a job. And he'd seen the way they looked at each other. But he couldn't help the way he felt. He'd do anything for the strawberry-blond mermaid who swam through his dreams.

He wasn't brave enough to use her name, but decided to leave a copy of the song he wrote for Amy with her things. She'd find it in the morning. If she liked him at all, she'd realize the song was about her and let him know she returned his feelings. If not, he'd just pretend he'd written the song for someone else.

That would work.

It was dark, but the back doors were open, so Jeff could see well enough to find Amy's cubby and put her stuff inside. Decision made, he placed the flash drive on top, taped to a note he'd worked on for hours at home.

New song—let me know what you think, the note said.

He hoped that sounded nonchalant enough.

Maybe Dennis and Gina were out on the deck or had to check on the otter pool or something. He walked through the open doorway, leaned over the railing.

"Gina, Dennis, anybody here?"

No one answered. Straightening up, he turned to go back into the lab, then froze. Something straight out of a sci-fi nightmare loomed between him and the safety of the lab. A faceless, alien monster stood before him. Darth Vader in a suit.

Jeff was suddenly acutely aware of everything.

"What do you want?" he asked, pressing himself back against the railing. "I don't have any money," he yelled, throwing his car keys at him. "Here! Take my car—it's in the parking lot."

The monster didn't answer.

Jeff turned and raced down the metal stairs, taking two at a time, but the monster stayed right behind him.

Nothing personal, kid.

30

Amy turned south onto PCH. She'd spent the afternoon and early evening at Fashion Island doing prewedding shopping, just like she'd promised her mom when she borrowed the car. She really *was* doing wedding shopping, just not with Liam like she said, and not all day.

She did find some cool stuff, but everything she liked was really expensive. The thought of being Liam's wife filled her with joy, but the actual details of planning a wedding were proving to be a little overwhelming.

Traffic was heavy in both directions, but steady. The radio said a storm was coming in, but for now, the coast basked in the last rays of an afternoon sun. Everything from highway to hills glowed warm, reflecting a crimson and tangerine sky. To her right, the sun flooded the ocean with liquid mango.

She couldn't wait to get to the center. She needed some Sadie time! Amy had long since given up thinking of the orphaned sea otter pup as Otter 1, though she kept up the pretext around

Gina. She had an idea Dennis knew she wasn't following all the rules, but so far he hadn't ratted her out.

In order not to arouse suspicion, she would only have about an hour with her little pup. Gina and Dennis were down in La Jolla checking out a stranded otter—a possible new resident for SSOS, a friend for Sadie, she hoped—but they might decide to drive back today, instead of spending the night down there. If they did stay overnight, Gina would make arrangements for one of the other volunteers to cover the night shift, so she didn't have much time.

When she arrived, it was just dark, but a few small security lights lined the gravel road that led to the main parking lot.

Telling her mom she was doing some registry selections with Liam and Liam she was going wedding dress shopping with her mom was a brilliant plan. With only five reminders to drive safely and be sure to push the clutch in all the way before shifting, her mom finally handed her the keys to Lola for the afternoon and evening. Her mom said she was doing some work in her studio anyway and wouldn't need to drive anywhere. Her mom had seemed pretty distracted. Apparently there was some kind of funding problem. Her mom would straighten it out. She always did.

Liam was happily ensconced in his dining table office at their rental cottage, writing a journal article on the local kelp-bed restoration project he'd been working on with Tava'e's cousins. He hoped to publish it soon.

Normally a truthful person, Amy only felt slightly guilty about this deception. She just couldn't think of any other way to get some time alone with Sadie. From the minute she looked in the orphaned sea otter pup's eyes, a fierce flood of warmth surged through her body. She'd never known such a primal, instinctive protectiveness and love.

Logically, she knew the ultimate goal of every sea otter pup rescue was release back into the wild, but they just built this beautiful aquarium. They had a whole empty sea otter paradise here! Why shouldn't Sadie have the benefit of leading a long, safe life versus being thrown back into the ocean, which was full of sharks and crazy people on boats with outboard motors and pollution!

Still, her conscience nagged. Was she doing it for herself, or for Sadie?

Pushing those thoughts to the back of her mind, she got out of the car. Dark clouds meant rain was on the horizon, though they were still a ways out. She wasn't going to be long, but she left the top up anyway, just in case. Anyone raised in a beach town knew weather changed quickly. And her mom's car had leather seats.

Faint thunder sounded in the distance. The air smelled like rain. She let herself inside.

Wanting to save a few minutes by taking the elevator directly down to level 1 versus going in the side entrance, which was farther from the elevator, Amy parked in the main parking lot by the fountain. Gina gave them all keys to the main entrance so she or Dennis didn't have to keep coming up to get them every time.

Sadie's favorite food was shrimp. The little otter had graduated from Dennis's clam shakes last week and, ever since, ate a healthy amount of shellfish every day. All Sadie's food was now stored on level 1 in the large freezers and refrigerators that would feed all the residents once they were fully stocked.

When she turned right at the T to park in the main lot, Amy noticed a big black sedan next to the employee entrance. Gina must have gotten a new car. Weird. Didn't seem her style. She didn't peg Gina for a major boat car. That was something old people drove.

Looked like they took the Jeep down to La Jolla. Maybe

that meant they would bring the injured otter back and Sadie would have someone to play with once it was nursed back to health. If it was a mature female, maybe she could even act as a surrogate mother. Gina said Sadie would need an older female otter to teach her how to be a sea otter. Amy wished she could change into a sea otter so she could show Sadie how to dive, find shellfish, roll over, and groom her fur perfectly.

Only in Disney movies.

Level 1 was dark. Dungeon-like on a good day, tonight it was definitely spooky with no one around, so Amy didn't waste any time. Filling one of the plastic buckets halfway up with a healthy shrimp snack for Sadie, she shut the freezer and hit the "Up" arrow for the elevator. The light was on a timer and would go off in a few seconds. Inside, she pressed the button and impatiently waited for the ding signaling her arrival at level 2, where her charge was housed. It arrived with a clunk before the doors opened.

Eeeeee! Eeeeeee!

Nothing wrong with Sadie's ears. Amy's little sea otter knew that ding meant company, and usually, company meant food. Not bothering to go back to her cubby to change clothes or don the mask and poncho outfit, Amy turned right into the otter tank room where Sadie was waiting for her, calling at the top of her little lungs.

"Hey, little girl! Hungry?" Amy said, reaching into the bucket with the scoop for some shrimp. Her charge was definitely hungry.

It was past dinner time, and she was getting hungry herself. She wouldn't have minded sharing Sadie's shrimp if they came cooked, shelled, and with a little cocktail sauce on the side.

The baby otter polished off several scoops of her favorite food in no time, then dove back into the water to roll around with pleasure and play with her toys.

Last week, Dennis hooked up a mini basketball hoop on the side of her pool, and the sleek little animal delighted in dunking the rubber ball whenever possible. It gave her additional exercise and was often used for older otters who had arthritis, Gina explained, to keep them flexible and reduce joint pain.

Amy looked up at the clock. She still had a little time. By the sound of the waves, the storm was picking up, but it didn't sound too strong yet. No lightning or thunder. Maybe it would just rain. A little water wouldn't hurt an otter—or her.

"Hey, little girl, how would you like to go in the big pool?"

When Sadie didn't react, she added some excitement to her voice and opened her eyes wide. "Big pool!"

Sadie didn't understand the words, but Amy's tone of voice told her something fun was being suggested, and otters are all about fun. She swam quickly to the edge and hauled herself out onto the rubber mat, eager for the next adventure of the night. Amy was definitely more fun than her usual babysitters.

Amy did a quick but thorough towel dry—she had learned that much—and coaxed Sadie into the cat carrier they used to transport her down to the lab for bloodwork and weighing or down the outside stairs to the lower deck. The training pool set up on a cement slab was about the only thing on that level. Beyond that was just the sand and water of the cove enclosed by rock on each side.

"If you keep eating like a little pig, I'll have to rename you Wilbur, and I won't be able to carry you to the pool anymore," she said. "You'll have to learn to waddle down these stairs all by yourself!"

31

Amy hesitated as she stepped out onto the narrow deck. The wind was louder out here, and she smelled rain in the air.

She couldn't see much but knew there was a floodlight by the pool. Once she got down there, they'd be fine. There was a switch by the entrance to the pool area, and in the meantime, she could hang on to the railing with one hand and see well enough not to fall down the steep metal stairs.

Growing impatient for release, Sadie started moving around in her carrier, verbally complaining as soon as they reached the bottom of the stairs. The wind began whipping Amy's hair across her face. Not in her usual work mode, she hadn't pulled it back into a scrunchie or braided it down her back like she usually did.

Thinking more each moment that this wasn't such a great idea, she quickly circled around the left of the above-ground pool. She felt better when she reached the gate and located the light switch on the side.

She would just let Sadie in the pool for a few minutes, scoop her out, and get back upstairs in plenty of time before the storm hit. She already felt guilty about lying to her mom and to Liam.

As she reached out with her right hand and flipped the switch on, she felt something behind her, and before she could turn around to see what it was, a large hand clamped down on her wrist.

A slice of terror stabbed her gut. Fighting panic, keeping a grip on Sadie's carrier, she wrenched around, jabbing blindly with her elbow while simultaneously stomping down on what she hoped was her attacker's instep. She couldn't decide whether to hit him in the head with the carrier or try to smash his throat with her elbow. She couldn't get the carrier high enough anyway, with Sadie in it, so both missed, but her foot made a satisfying, solid connection. Maybe even a crunch. She didn't know if it would stop him, but maybe it would slow him down.

Her mom's friend, Iona Slatterly, head of security at the arts festival in town, had taught them all some basic defense moves. Iona was tough and made sure all the first-year summer hires knew how to protect themselves when walking to their cars at night in the big, empty parking lot in the back of the festival grounds. Right now, Amy wished she had practiced more.

She couldn't see the man's face, backlit by the floodlight, and he was wearing one of the welding masks. His suit flapped, snapping like ersatz sails as the wind whipped around in the compact cove. His shirt was plastered to his chest with rain, which was coming down harder now, and his leather dress shoes couldn't make good purchase on the wet cement. He fell back from her unexpected response but quickly regained his balance. Spreading his arms, he effectively cut off her only avenue of escape, the stairs.

DEVIL'S CLAW

The crash of the waves was deafening this close to shore, amplified by the acoustics of the cove.

Behind the man, at the foot of the stairs, Amy saw someone lying on the cold cement, half-in and half-out of the light.

Jeff! Was that Jeff?

Something black seeped from his head, across the cement, disappearing into the inky shadows beyond the reach of the security light.

She had no idea if he was still alive, but she knew the only way she was going to help Jeff was to find a way to escape.

But there was no way out.

Quickly, she assessed her surroundings. So far, the man in the mask hadn't resumed his attack, but just stood there, between her and the stairs, as if trying to decide if she was worth killing or not.

Devil's Claw rose a good forty feet to her right. Another, smaller rock formation fashioned the opposite edge of the cove, but she knew she'd never reach it in time, let alone be able to climb over it in the rain and dark while hauling a screaming sea otter.

The storm had arrived, and with it, slashing rain.

There was no time to think of other options. At the next crack of thunder, Amy turned and bolted toward the cove. If she was going to die, she was going to die trying. If she could make it past the breakwater, she knew she could swim south, around Devil's Claw, parallel to shore, until she got to Main Beach and help. At least, she hoped so. She wasn't in swimming shape.

She hoped the monster behind her couldn't swim at all.

Brave, but not stupid, she looked for her best shot. She'd have to time it just right, or she and Sadie would never make it.

Powerful waves smashed up the side of Devil's Claw, sending white spray straight up and white foam sliding back down, to be sucked powerfully out to sea, rushing right back in again, to a soundtrack of howling winds. Mother Nature was truly impressive.

How was she supposed to get past that without being completely mashed and broken on the rocks?

Out of the corner of her eye, she saw a shape that didn't fit. A rounded lump of light gray with a black stripe.

The Zodiac! She'd never seen a more beautiful sight.

She had no idea if she could get the motor started or if it even had any gas in it, but it was better than swimming. One of Solange's supporters had donated the raft to the center. It was an older model you had to start like a lawn mower versus just pushing a button.

Any raft in a storm, right?

"Hang on, Sadie!"

Hoping she could outrun her assailant, Amy splashed right into the cold water, sprinting toward the Zodiac, half expecting a strong hand to grab her shoulder and yank her back at any minute.

Saltwater stung her eyes and made it hard to find a good spot to board the inflatable. Grabbing on to the rope that ran around the top of the raft, she hoisted Sadie's carrier in first, then, using the ropes on the side, hauled herself up and scrambled in.

This wasn't a Junior Guard test or drill. This was for real. Shaking with cold and terror, she unsnapped one of the oars and pushed off from the rocks to put as much distance as possible between herself and her attacker. Risking a quick look back over her shoulder, she didn't see him anywhere. Was he in the water?

DEVIL'S CLAW

Sadie's screams were heart wrenching, but she couldn't stop to comfort the little otter now, or they were both dead.

Wind and rain lashing her face, almost knocking her out of the raft, she pushed against the rocks on her left to get clear, then dug in deep with the paddle. Incoming waves got bigger. One of them threw her back against the rocks, scraped her arm, slicing her from shoulder to elbow. Saltwater seared into the open wound, causing her to cry out. Securing Sadie's carrier as best she could in the bottom of the raft, Amy crawled to the back of the Zodiac and focused on getting the motor started. Hoping it was idiot proof, she yanked on the cord.

Nothing.

Was there a button you pushed first, or did you pull one time all the way, or several short pulls to prime the engine? She just couldn't remember. It took several tries, but by some miracle, the engine turned over and she aimed the raft toward open sea. Even then, it took every ounce of energy and concentration she had to keep the raft from being flipped or shredded on the rocks. She couldn't see Sadie but could definitely hear her. So far, the carrier was staying in the boat.

Fighting the power of the storm surge, avoiding being forced onto the rocks again, it took what seemed like forever to clear the last outcropping of Devil's Claw, but finally, to her left, Amy saw the lights of Main Beach. She could barely keep Sadie's cage in the raft and the raft on course. If there was enough gas, she was pretty sure she could make it to the relative safety of the long stretch of open beach on the other side.

If they did run out of gas, there were some small sea caves on that side, too. One of them might be high enough for her and Sadie to wait out the storm, but she had to get help for Jeff as soon as possible, so waiting out the storm really wasn't an option. She willed herself not to think of his still form or the life oozing out of it.

Her mind flooded with mounting panic. Why hadn't she thought this through? What was she thinking, taking this tiny, vulnerable animal out when a storm was coming? Why did she always do such idiotic things?

And it didn't help that Sadie wouldn't shut up! If only she would just stop screaming, Amy could think! There had to be a way out of the mess she'd gotten herself into. Of course, she couldn't have anticipated being attacked, but if she hadn't lied and taken Sadie out when she wasn't supposed to, none of this would have happened.

Main Beach was only about a mile south. If they could make land safely, she could get help. She could make it to her mom's. She would know what to do.

"Don't worry, Sadie, I've got you!" she said, wishing she felt as confident as she was trying to sound.

Pushing Sadie's carrier down as far as it would go, holding it in place with her foot, Amy grabbed the tiller and looked up. Where was the moon? At first she thought the storm clouds were blotting out the moon and stars. Her stomach fell as she realized what she was seeing.

Gathering itself into a huge swell, the power of the Pacific Ocean was racing toward them.

And all that was behind them was the unforgiving reach of Devil's Claw.

32

SATURDAY, JULY 25, 2015

Logan looked at the front door again, avoiding the temptation to get up and see if Amy was back yet. She'd already checked three times. Getting up again would only make her admit to herself how worried she was. Besides, staring at the empty driveway wouldn't make Amy get there any sooner.

The storm outside swirled around her home, alternately buffeting the walls and whispering secrets down the chimney. Even with the winds picking up, she would have heard Lola's reassuring growl if her daughter did pull up.

Another fifteen minutes passed.

"She should be back by now," Logan said, standing.

Giving in to her anxiety, she opened her front door and peered into the darkness. No Lola. The storm rewarded her motherly concern with a slap of rain across her face before she could close the door again and stalk back to the couch.

"Malls don't have windows," Bonnie said, nudging deeper into the cushions, glass of wine in hand. "She's probably lost in a delicious flurry of wedding dresses and cupcake sampling. Mere thunderstorms mean nothing to a young girl in love."

Scowling, Logan didn't look convinced.

"Liam's with her," Bonnie added. "If they did get caught in the storm coming back, Liam would use good sense and pull over. If there's one thing that boy is, it's responsible. They're probably tucked into that Thai place Amy likes, making goo-goo eyes at each other, completely oblivious to the weather."

"You're probably right." Logan looked at her phone. "I'll give them another thirty minutes," she said. "If they're not back by 10:00, I'll call Rick."

"You've already called the hospital and the highway patrol, what do you think Rick can do?"

"I don't know, exactly," she said, getting up to pace. "This is new territory. I never had to worry about Amy. I never had to call the police to track her down. She never gave me a lick of trouble. Never stayed out late. Didn't drink. Didn't do drugs. Got good grades, used common sense. Well, not always . . . I don't think going to Africa exhibited very much common sense . . ."

Logan was rambling now, and knew it. She looked over at Bonnie, who had become uncharacteristically subdued. Curled on the couch, Bonnie took a small sip of her wine, looking down into the glass. All Logan could see was the top of her friend's thick mop of blond curls.

About an hour ago, Bonnie had shown up with enough Mexican takeout for an army. She'd stopped by Juan's on the way down.

"Girls night in!" Bonnie announced upon arrival.

The twins were at Outdoor Science Camp, and Mike had taken the girls to see the new *Muppets Most Wanted* movie for a daddy/daughter date.

Her timing couldn't have been better.

Logan had been at it all day, either on her computer or on the phone—trying to solve the funding issue for Fractals. Ben was visiting his sister, so she'd worked straight through dinner. She was ready for a break.

Mrs. Houser's children were not as generous as their mother had been and were fighting to cut off all outgoing monies from their mother's estate, including those promised to Fractals. Not wanting to fight with children whose mother had just died, Logan was combing the Internet for other funding sources.

She'd located several good possibilities online, but when she got through on the phone, they inevitably regretted to inform her that "due to the economic downturn, those grant funds are no longer available. We will of course keep your contact information should things change in the near future . . . blah, blah, blah." Fractals wouldn't have a future if they didn't get some cash now.

Where were all the wealthy one percenters when you needed them? Why weren't they funding programs like Fractals? They could fund a thousand music/math programs and not feel it! It was so frustrating.

Logan pulled her mind back from worrying about Amy and Fractals long enough to focus on Bonnie. Why had she gotten silent? And why was she avoiding eye contact?

And then it hit her. Of course . . .

Haley. Here she was, going on about how good Amy was, what a model daughter, when she knew Bonnie and Mike had been having a tough time with their always-in-trouble fifteen-year-old, Haley. Logan sat back down on the couch, put her phone on the coffee table, turned sideways, and tucked one leg under her.

"Hey . . . I'm sorry—I forgot," she said. "Talk to me."

Something unraveled in Bonnie, and tears poured down her cheeks in quiet streams.

"Haley got arrested. Mike had to bail her out of jail."

"Jeez, I had no idea it had gotten that bad," Logan said. "What did she get arrested for?"

"Drinking and driving—she got a DUI," Bonnie said dully. Then, her voice level rising with anxiety, she added, "DUIs don't just go away. Even if she gets off with community service because it's her first time, it will go on her record, and she just doesn't seem to understand how bad this is, how close she is to ruining her life! Let alone the fact that she could get hurt—or even worse—hurt or even kill someone else! She seemed more upset at getting caught than understanding what she'd done."

Logan had a zillion questions, but stayed quiet. They'd been friends for so long she knew she just needed to listen, not jump in or give advice. Bonnie just needed to talk it out.

"She goes to court next week. We've hired her an attorney, but she's going to pay back every cent of that money."

"Sounds fair to me," Logan said.

"She has some money from her summer job. She was saving up for a car, but now . . ."

Finally, when Bonnie let it all out, Logan got up, got her a box of tissues, and gave her a fierce hug before sitting back down.

Bonnie fell back into one of the big pillows. A determined look came over her face.

"We're not going to bail her out again," she said, "she knows that. Tough love and all that. I know it's the right thing to do, but it's so *hard* . . . The consequences are so much bigger now. I just hope she gets it together before something really bad happens." Bonnie scrunched her shoulders up to her ears, then let them drop. "Huh!" She exhaled, then looked at Logan and smiled. That was Bonnie for you. Feel it, deal with it, then move on.

Logan wished she could do that. Emotions had always come easily to Bonnie. Logan was just beginning to figure all that out. She was getting there but couldn't even express her true feelings for Ben to herself, yet—let alone to Ben.

She wanted to say something reassuring or promise everything was going to be all right, but honesty was the best thing she could come up with. She didn't lie to friends or children, so she told her the truth.

"You and Mike are great parents. You've given Haley a solid foundation. You're doing all the right things. You're giving her the chance to grow up. It's going to be up to Haley. If it's any consolation, I think she's a great kid."

For now, the best gift she could give her friend was moral support.

With Bonnie's crisis dealt with, Logan's mind turned back to Amy. She checked, but there was still no message or missed call on her phone.

Where was she?

At Bonnie's suggestion, she tried the Thai restaurant, but no one had seen them there. The mall was closed.

"Of course!" Logan said, jumping off the couch and racing toward the front door.

She started pulling on her shoes, tossing Bonnie's back to her for her to put on.

Bonnie obeyed, assuming Logan would explain why they were getting ready to go out in a storm.

"The only thing between here and the mall that's not residential or open coast along that stretch of state park is the sea otter center," she said. "Amy loves that little otter."

"Yep, I bet she stopped off for a visit," Bonnie agreed.

"Maybe they got stuck when the storm hit—they're probably there now, just waiting it out."

"That doesn't explain why she didn't call, though . . . ," Logan said.

Simultaneously jumping off the couch, Bonnie grabbed her keys, Logan yanked open the door, and they raced into the slanting rain toward Bonnie's SUV.

Mothers united!

33

SATURDAY, JULY 25, 2015

The storm quickly muted when they climbed in Bonnie's Toyota Highlander. No one was on the road, so Bonnie had no trouble making good time up PCH.

The Friends of the Sea Otter sign at the entrance looked anything but friendly in the harsh glare of the headlights. Thanks to the storm, the narrow road in had turned into a pockmarked obstacle course, slick with rain. Navigating without streetlights didn't help, but they made it to the gravel parking lot without sliding into a ditch.

Almost giddy with relief, Logan saw Lola parked out in front.

She took a deep breath. Now she could get mad.

"Amy's cell phone better have been eaten by aliens," she said as she launched herself out of the car, digging in her purse for the keys.

Bonnie laughed as she clicked the door locks on and ran with Logan in the rain toward the building.

"She probably just forgot to charge it," Bonnie said as she shook out her jacket when they got there.

That doesn't explain why she couldn't have used Liam's phone, though . . . , Logan thought.

Just then, her own phone rang.

It was Liam. She needed to stay calm and not yell at him. He probably had a perfectly reasonable explanation for not calling when Amy's phone died.

"Liam, thanks for calling, we just pulled up. I figured Amy probably talked you into making a pit stop to play with Otter 1."

"What? Where are you?" Liam asked. "Isn't Amy with you? I was calling to make sure you guys were okay in case you were driving back in the storm. I thought you were wedding dress shopping."

Logan tried to sound calm.

"No, Liam, she's not with me. She borrowed my car and said she was with you. Bonnie and I are at sea otter center now. The car's here—I'm sure she's inside."

They'd reached the front entrance, and Logan was unlocking the door. The repairs were finished a week ago.

"I'll have Amy call you as soon as we get inside. I'm sure her phone just died or she's someplace inside that doesn't get reception. Don't worry," Logan said. "We'll call you in a few."

She, however, was definitely worried. None of this made sense. With a growing uneasy feeling in the pit of her stomach, Logan got into the elevator with Bonnie and pushed the button for the lab on level 2.

Logan stepped out first. She looked around, but nothing seemed out of the ordinary. The back door was open for fresh air, and Gina's purse was on the stainless steel surface of the island in the middle of the lab. Then Logan remembered that

Gina and Dennis had driven to La Jolla. Why would they leave the door open?

And that wasn't Gina's purse.

Logan and Bonnie could hear faint wheezing sounds coming from the other side of the lab. Bonnie flipped on the light, and Logan raced around the table, toward the sounds.

Solange Sauvage lay crumpled on the floor, barely breathing. Except for the ugly bruises on her throat, she could have been sleeping.

Who would want to hurt Solange?

"Call nine one one!"

Ignoring the dispatcher's instructions to stay put until help arrived, Logan began searching for Amy. There was nothing they could do for Solange other than make sure she didn't move until the ambulance got there.

"I've got this," Bonnie said, shooing her away. "Go! Find Amy!"

The obvious first place to look was Otter 1's nursery tank room, but it was empty.

"Damn!" Logan muttered.

Hoping beyond hope that Amy had not been foolish enough to take the little otter out in the storm, but needing to check all possibilities, Logan found a flashlight hanging on one of the pegboards on the wall by the exit, went through the open doors, and began clanging down the stairs, fighting against the wind. Barely able to hold on to the railing and keep the flashlight in the other hand, she was almost at the bottom before she saw him.

"Jeff!"

The young man lay flat on the cement. Rain pelted his body, plastering jet-black hair to his forehead, down which pink, watery rivulets, tainted with what must be his blood, shimmered in the beam of the flashlight.

"Oh my God!"

Logan stumbled the rest of the way down.

Although he was obviously dead, she reached out and felt for a pulse. Nothing. Cold to the touch. Disbelief flooded through her. He couldn't be dead. He was too young!

She tried again. She was shaking. Maybe he was still alive. She couldn't feel even a flicker. She held her breath in case her own breathing was preventing her from discerning his. Still nothing.

Why? Why would anyone want to hurt these two people? There was no money to steal, no reason for anyone to do this.

Logan's first thought was to administer CPR, but she knew enough not to risk rolling him over in case his neck or back was injured. She shouted up to Bonnie to let dispatch know they had another victim. She couldn't bring herself to say body.

Bonnie waved over the railing to let her know she heard and ducked back inside to stay with Solange.

Nothing else she could do for Jeff until the EMTs arrived, Logan ran around the pool enclosure, hoping to find Amy and Otter 1 somehow safe and sound, huddled inside against the rain.

The floodlight was on, but the interior was empty.

Panic rising, not knowing where else to look, she jumped off the small rock wall at the edge of the otter pool, onto the short, crescent beach, and ran toward the water. She couldn't achieve more than a knee squat without getting knocked down by the wind, so she crawled over the rocks tumbling off Devil's Claw, searching for any sign of Amy or Otter 1.

Then she saw what else was missing. The raft. There was usually a Zodiac raft tucked back here, tied to a metal ring drilled into one of the larger rocks. Gina always kept it down here.

Was it possible that Amy had taken out the inflatable? Why would she do that in a storm? And did Amy even know how to use it? Did she go before the storm and then get caught in it? She wouldn't take the otter out—she knew that the pup was nowhere near ready to be released back into the wild.

The only explanation that made sense was that her fragile daughter, still not completely recovered from her bout with malaria, had escaped whatever evil had happened here at the center, only to be thrust into a roiling, angry Pacific Ocean, alone and adrift with a baby sea otter in the middle of a raging storm.

"Bonnie!" Logan yelled as she scrambled back over the rock wall and raced up the stairs. "Bonnie!"

The emergency services dispatcher couldn't believe she was getting a third call from the same number. At least this time it was not for another injured or possibly deceased person, but a missing one.

A call was put in to the Coast Guard.

She hated to see them have to go out in weather like this, but that's what they trained for. If a missing girl was out there, they'd find her.

34

A uniformed officer Logan recognized, a friend of Rick's, nodded to her from across the room but kept at his assigned task, cordoning off the lab with yellow crime-scene tape. She and Bonnie had been placed on two of the tall stools in the hallway, instructed not to touch anything. She felt like she'd been sent to the principal's office.

Every corner and cupboard on every floor, as well as the surrounding grounds, had been searched. Twice. No Amy. No otter. All clear.

Except her daughter was still missing.

Logan stared across the lab to what she could see of the storm outside. Her body clenched. The Coast Guard already had one helicopter in the air and a cutter on its way.

"They're going to find her, Logan," Bonnie said. Bonnie had no compunctions about lying if it would comfort her friend.

A small community, Jasper only had two homicide detectives. She and Bonnie were instructed to stay glued to their stools until they arrived. Rick called and reassured her every cop in Jasper was looking for Amy. In the meantime, Logan reached Ben as he was driving back from a job in South County. He sensed it was more important to organize a search party for Amy than come hold Logan's hand. He and Liam were both down at Tava'e's doing exactly that.

Through Tava'e's infamous coconut telegraph, half of Jasper was calling in or showing up to volunteer their services. Sally and Ned, Taylor, Amosa, they were all there. The only person not there was Brandon. She'd asked Ben to hold off contacting him until she could call him herself and tell him about Jeff. He was going to be devastated. They had been friends since kindergarten.

A possible double murder didn't happen every day in Jasper. One victim was definitely dead, the second, an elderly woman, in critical condition at the hospital. The coroner would do the initial intake. The case didn't merit a medical examiner, but LA was sending an extra crime-scene tech to assist in processing the scene. Jasper's tech, Esturban, who operated as a crew of one, had started but was grateful for the eminent arrival of reinforcements.

No one had yet brought Jeff's body up from the deck below, although they'd taken some blue plastic tarp down, forming a rain tent over that area. Logan blinked back tears and tried not to see the stark image of the young man's white face or the rain hitting his unblinking eyes. She squeezed her own eyes tightly shut and tried to shake away the memory.

Solange, though barely breathing, was still alive. At least, she was when they rolled her out. The EMTs had very gently placed the tiny woman on the gurney and taken her down the elevator to the waiting ambulance. Logan didn't know what Solange would want, but just before the elevator doors closed, she reached in and gave one of the EMTs a piece of paper with

Scott Dekker's name. She didn't have his number or know where he was staying, but someone would be able to track him down.

If he really was Solange's half brother, he was her only living relative and should at least be informed what had happened.

While they were waiting for the detectives, one of the officers had fired up a coffee machine somewhere and brought them each a cup. Bonnie only drank tea, but Logan numbly accepted the gift, if only to give her hands something to do.

When the detectives finally arrived, she recognized one of them from two summers ago. She'd seen Detective Andrews from a distance, inside a glassblowers' cage, just steps from the broken body of a young woman who'd been brutally murdered. Tall. Black hair. Same white shirt, suit, and dress shoes. Didn't the man ever wear jeans and tennis shoes?

He hadn't seen her that day, because she was, as usual, someplace she wasn't supposed to be, digging for information she wasn't supposed to have, in order to help clear her friend, Thomas, suspected of killing the girl.

Logan remembered Detective Andrews's monosyllabic efficiency when talking with Iona, the coroner, and other witnesses. She hoped he was as competent as he seemed.

Now that the shock was wearing off, she felt angry. Angry at whoever murdered Jeff, attacked Solange, and terrified her daughter into the Pacific Ocean during a violent storm.

But right now, all she wanted was to find Amy. Alive and well, preferably with a baby sea otter in tow.

She went over her conversation with the Coast Guard officer who'd called her as soon as the dispatcher made the initial report.

"Yes, she is most probably in a Zodiac inflatable. No, I don't know the exact size, but it's gray with a black stripe,

I think . . . Yes, it has a motor . . . the kind you start like a lawnmower . . . Registered to a Gina—I can't think of her last name right now—she's the director of the sea otter center here, if rafts—inflatable boats—are registered, I don't know!"

She was rambling again.

Fighting to remain calm and answer the nice officer's questions, Logan slowed down. She understood it was dangerous for the Coast Guard to go out in a storm, and that the officer wanted to make sure there was a good reason to do so, that Amy was actually out on the ocean, in need of rescue, and not cooling her heels in a coffee shop or bar somewhere after a fight with her boyfriend.

"Yes, she left before the storm to do some shopping . . . said she'd be back tonight."

She neglected to add that Amy had not told her the total truth about this particular shopping trip.

"No, she didn't give an exact time. No, she didn't say she was going to go to the sea otter center, but she must have since the car was there. No, she's never done this before. This isn't some runaway teenager. My daughter is twenty-four years old. No, for the umpteenth time, her fiancé hasn't seen her, either, and they didn't get into a fight."

Finally, the officer had agreed to instigate a full-on search for one Amy McKenna, twenty-four-year-old female, alone in an inflatable raft, missing since approximately 5:00 p.m. or later, somewhere in the vicinity of the rock outcropping at the north end of Jasper's Main Beach, known as Devil's Claw.

In light of the facts that her daughter was missing and he knew Rick, Detective Andrews only took brief initial interviews from Bonnie and Logan before letting them go, with firm promises to show up first thing in the morning to give complete, formal statements at the station.

DEVIL'S CLAW

When finally released by the police, Bonnie and Logan practically raced to Bonnie's car. After they'd called Liam to tell him where they were going, Logan pulled up GPS on her phone and plugged in their destination: Newport Beach Coast Guard Station. It was the one that handled rescues for this area, she discovered, and the one from where the search helicopter launched.

After he'd gathered the information he needed about Amy, the Coast Guard commander told Logan in no uncertain terms that she was to wait at home, but that wasn't going to happen.

35

Lashed by increasingly furious winds, more rain than Logan had seen in years sheeted down the massive bay windows on the observation deck of the Coast Guard station. That and the complete absence of any starlight or moonlight prevented them from seeing anything outside. She and Bonnie had been relegated to the visitor's section, while all the main action was taking place downstairs in the control room.

She wished she hadn't come. She was just about to suggest they go back to Tava'e's to help Ben and Liam with the search when a junior officer poked his head around the door.

"They've spotted her, ma'am," he said, and then quickly corrected himself. "At least, they spotted a raft and what they think is someone who might be your daughter back up in one of the sea caves, near your daughter's last known location. The spotlight caught a corner of some clothing. Could you verify what color clothing she was wearing?" He waited for her answer, holding his breath.

Logan tried to focus, thinking back to this afternoon, which seemed light-years away.

"Green! Lime green!" she shouted.

Amy was wearing a lime-green North Face T-shirt and some shorts when she left this afternoon. Logan bought her that T-shirt up in Portland, Oregon, last year.

"Bingo!" He grinned and raced back upstairs.

Logan's eyes leaked with relief, and she accepted a gripping hug from Bonnie. They'd found her, but now they had to somehow get her on board the helicopter and bring her home. She tried not to imagine her daughter injured or worse.

They heard the young man shouting to someone as he took the stairs two at a time, back down to the control center.

"OK! Mom verified—bright-green T-shirt . . ."

The rest of his conversation was lost to them, but Logan resisted the urge to race after him. They needed to do whatever it was they did to bring Amy home—she would only be in the way.

Waiting is harder than doing.

Everything about an ocean rescue is loud. The howling winds, the crashing waves, the rotary blades, the engine. All communication between pilot, copilot, rescue swimmer, and other personnel was done through headsets. But they were there. They'd spotted the girl and were now in position.

Twenty feet below, the sea roiled and churned. Both the pilot and the rescue swimmer eyed the sea cave where the girl was last seen, calibrating the power of the waves surging in and out. He'd have to time it just right.

"Swimmer One, Swimmer One, be advised, we've got twelve minutes to get this done . . ."

DEVIL'S CLAW

Kevin nodded and got in position. A former high school swim team captain, he was all lean muscle and long limbs. This was his seventeenth rescue, but only his second sea cave. Extending powerful legs punctuated by long black swim fins out the open copter door, keeping perfect form, he jumped. Just another day at the office.

"Swimmer out the door," the pilot radioed in while the copilot kept them in sight, hovering above where Kevin had entered the water, keeping a spotlight on the churning surface. He trusted the pilot. His job was to not get knocked out of the sky, to be there to pull him up, hopefully with a passenger.

Kevin's head, now nothing more than a tiny orange dot to the pilot, bobbed up and down in the dark water, suspended momentarily, waiting for the next surge. When it came, he struck out: long strokes and powerful kicks—swimming for all he was worth, and then he was gone, sucked into the mouth of the cave, and all the pilot could do was wait.

It was much quieter inside. His headlight dimly lit rough, wet walls that formed a low-ceilinged cave. Deep, but shallow, it came to a point somewhere in the back. About twenty feet in, on a narrow slab of slippery basalt, he saw the girl. She sat, huddled, shivering, and soaked, staring into space. A few freckles stood out against her white skin. Long strands of wet hair made her look like a mermaid. But mermaids didn't shiver like that.

He needed to hurry. If she wasn't already hypothermic, she would be soon. Incoming waves, although not as powerful as the ones outside, slapped against her perch, threatening to pull her off. Blood trickled down her left arm. After a quick visual inspection for other injuries, following protocol, he identified himself while still in the water.

"Hello, Amy, my name is Kevin Reid, and I'm here to help you. Are you OK? Are you injured?"

Instead of answering his questions, she looked around as if just realizing someone was there and said, "Sadie . . . Where's Sadie?"

Kevin clicked on his radio and checked with his pilot. "Just one soul, right?"

"Yes, one twenty-four-year-old female," the pilot reassured him, named Amy, not Sadie.

Trauma made people say all kinds of things that didn't make any sense. Approaching with caution, knowing he didn't have the luxury of time, he made the decision not to look for someone named Sadie, who obviously wasn't there, and proceeded with the rescue.

"It's okay, Amy, I'm going to get you out of here."

Pulling himself up on the ledge beside her, he gave her a quick check for broken bones, then, without much help or resistance from the young girl, who had gone silent again, slid her back into the water.

"I got you, Amy," he said.

This was where people panicked, but he needn't have worried. This girl was limp in his arms. Gripping her in a firm fireman's carry, he paddled to the mouth of the cave, waited for the next good rush, then swam like hell to the bright spot of hope waiting for them on the open ocean.

Sea cave rescues were tricky. But in any ocean rescue, things could go wrong. You counted on that helicopter, and thank God, it was there. Kevin smiled. The loud black-and-orange machine, shaped like a bottlenose dolphin, was there.

Salvation and hallelujah!

The pilot spotted him at the same time. An old-timer, he had over 150 rescues logged, but he was always relieved to see them make it out of those caves.

"Swimmer One, coming out!"

DEVIL'S CLAW

A gust of wind knocked the tail to the left, but the pilot got it steadied and began carefully lowering the large, rectangular, metal rescue basket.

In spite of the waves trying to tear the girl out of his grip, as soon as the basket was within reach, Kevin grabbed it and, as gently as possible, placed her inside, head resting on one orange cylinder, knees hanging over the other. Even sopping wet, she weighed almost nothing. Not talking at all now.

Thumbs-up, he signaled the pilot, then watched her being lifted to safety. Treading water, he waited his turn.

36

Somewhere around 2:30 a.m., Amy was discharged from the hospital. She'd been treated for hypothermia, and her vitals were good, but they'd insisted she wait for the results of a few more tests, *and* keep some dinner down first.

While they waited for an orderly, Detective Andrews came in. Apologizing for the intrusion, but not very sincerely, Logan thought, he asked Amy for a complete description of her attacker. He seemed almost disappointed the attack hadn't lasted longer so she could do a better job identifying him.

"Tall, maybe six feet? Could be shorter—he was wearing one of the welder's masks, and they cover everything. He was kind of stringy-looking, but strong . . ." Amy shivered involuntarily as she remembered the grip on her wrist. "No . . . I didn't hear his voice. He didn't say anything."

Finally, accepting the fact that his only conscious eye witness couldn't tell him more, Detective Andrews flipped his notebook shut, handed her his card, and told her to call if she remembered anything—any small detail might help. Said he'd be in touch.

Logan heard him asking the nurse at the desk if he could talk with Solange yet, but the nurse shook her head and looked at him like he was an idiot for asking. Solange was in the ICU, in critical condition.

Earlier, on their way to get Amy something to eat from the cafeteria—she requested tapioca pudding if they had it—they passed a nurse Ben knew from high school, one of his sister's friends. After introductions, Ben asked if she could find out anything about Solange's condition. The woman didn't mind bending the rules a bit for the hunk she'd always had a crush on.

She didn't work that floor but made a call on her cell. After getting the 411, she disconnected the call and slid her phone back into her pocket.

Talking only to Ben, she said, "Her trachea was bruised, but not crushed. She was able to breathe, but just barely until she got to the hospital. Given how long she was laying there getting very little oxygen, she may have sustained brain damage. They'll know more in twenty-four hours, when the swelling goes down."

With the heel of her hand, she pressed a pad on the wall, and a large door swung open. "She's one lucky woman," the nurse added over her shoulder, still ignoring Logan as she rushed off into a brightly lit corridor.

They didn't have tapioca, but Amy scarfed down the vanilla pudding they brought her as if she hadn't eaten all day, which, technically, she hadn't, if you don't count the hospital dinner of turkey, mashed potatoes and gravy, a roll, juice, and Jell-O she'd already inhaled.

Liam brought her some dry clothes, so as soon as they'd signed the papers and Amy was dressed, they wheeled her out to the main entrance. Hospital policy. Everybody had to leave via wheelchair. As they exited the elevator, Logan saw Scott Dekker walking in from the parking lot. He waited impatiently for the large automatic front doors to slide open, then hurried over to the front desk.

Good. They found him. And even better, he came.

Logan had a very hard time letting go of Amy's hand. Liam helped her into the car. All she needed now, the doctor said, was a good night's sleep and a few days' rest.

Physically, Amy was fine. Remarkably, other than a "gnarly" gash on the outside of her left arm, she escaped serious injury. But emotionally, she was still in shock. The news of Jeff's death hit her hard. Amy kept saying she just couldn't believe it. He was just a kid. How could he be dead?

Mixed with grief and shock was an emotion Amy wasn't vocalizing, but Logan saw it: her growing guilt over the loss of Otter 1. Logan didn't know what to say. She would just have to help her through it.

When trying to accurately relay the series of events for Detective Andrews, the last thing Amy said she remembered was the wall of water rolling over the raft, flipping it like a toothpick, knocking her and Sadie out of the raft. When she surfaced, neither the inflatable boat nor the carrier were anywhere to be seen. The rush of storm waves carried her toward shore, and eventually into one of the sea caves.

Ben drove Logan to pick up her car at the center, then dropped her off at her place. He needed to feed Purgatory and lock up, then he'd be over.

Tava'e's was dark when they drove past. The search party had long since packed up and gone home. She'd have to thank them all tomorrow. Or actually, she glanced at her watch, later today. And she'd have to call Brandon . . . She wondered if anyone had gotten ahold of Gina and Dennis.

The police would have notified Jeff's parents by now. She couldn't even imagine what they must be going through.

She made it as far as the couch, dropped her keys on the coffee table, and eased herself down into a prone position. Every part of her hurt.

She opened one eye and looked at the clock.

4:14 a.m.

Minutes or hours later, she sensed, more than felt, Ben's presence, lowering himself next to her on the couch. She managed to raise her heavy eyelids enough to see those blue eyes looking into hers. Without breaking the spell, he slowly traced a delicate line across her forehead, pushing a strand of hair away from her face, tucking it behind her ear, then let his hand drift down to cup her left breast.

She reached up and stroked the blond stubble on his cheek, then ran both hands across his chest and shoulders. He was deliciously warm.

The storm had passed, but he'd been there in the heart of it. He'd been there for her—in all the ways that mattered.

All the problems weren't fixed. All the puzzles weren't solved. But right now, all she wanted was to let go of it all, all those things she couldn't control. Just for now.

Stretching out along the length of his body, pulling him close, feeling the full warmth and weight of him, she intended to show Ben exactly how much he meant to her.

37

Much too early, the phone rang. It wasn't hers. Different ring-tone. Something by Blondie. Ben sat up and retrieved his phone from the dresser. The dresser was a hand-me-down from Bonnie. Logan still didn't own nightstands.

"Hello?"

Logan loved the sound of his morning voice. Burrowing back into the covers, she hoped he didn't have to go in to work and check on one of his job sites.

The room was really bright. What time was it, anyway?

Ben was listening to a long story by someone, so throwing off the covers, she raised her arms and stretched on tippy toes, then padded her way down the narrow stairs to the kitchen.

11:30 a.m. Wow.

They'd slept later than she thought.

Pouring a big tumbler of ice water, she took a long drink and looked out the window for Dimebox. He sat ramrod straight on a stump in the yard, tail flicking, eyes laser focused on a jewel-toned hummingbird flitting in and out of a flowering bush on the edge of Ben's lawn. Ruby-throated. Pretty.

Good luck with that, buddy.

The cat had been trying all summer but, as far as she knew, had yet to land one of the superfast, agile flyers.

She headed back upstairs, handing Ben the glass of water, along with a bottle of blood-pressure medicine he'd left on the kitchen counter.

She felt so wifely.

Too late to go back to bed, she went in her tiny bathroom and turned on the shower. She let the water run. It took forever for the hot water.

Ben was just finishing his call.

". . . OK, yes . . . I'll let her know. Thanks again for calling. Great news!" Ben said.

"Let me know what? What news?" Logan asked.

"That was Liam," he said. "He just called with some news from Amosa."

Ben's eyes sparkled.

Logan remembered Amosa—he had taken Liam out to work on the kelp beds.

"Make it a quick shower—in fact, I think we should take one together to save time. This is something you're going to want to see in person."

Ben loved secrets. He wouldn't tell her anything until they got in the car.

"Where are we going?" Logan asked.

"To the center. He grinned happily. They found Otter 1. Liam and Amy are on their way."

"You're kidding! Where? How? Is she OK?"

"Liam said they spotted her early this morning, wrapped up in some kelp, screaming her little lungs out. Other than being super hungry, she seemed to be okay. Amosa and his cousin found her when they went out to do their sea-urchin count. They called Gina. She did some first aid on her, said she was dehydrated, but other than that, came through her ordeal unscathed. Said it was a miracle the otter survived. She's at the center."

"Amazing, I can't believe it. That's fantastic news! I bet Amy went absolutely bonkers," Logan said.

She hoped Gina wouldn't be too angry with Amy for taking the otter out without permission. Yes, Amy was wrong to name the pup, wrong not to disguise herself with the mask and poncho, wrong to try to bond with a wild animal. Logan wondered if the otter would be able to be released back into the wild now. But Amy hadn't meant any harm. After all, she had just taken her down to the training pool. She hadn't meant to take the otter out into the open ocean. She hoped Gina would take into account Amy had been running away from a killer at the time.

Ben and Logan got to the center right behind Amy and Liam. Liam had made Amy eat breakfast first.

As Logan predicted, Amy was over-the-moon ecstatic that Otter 1—she was careful to call her by her assigned name now—was safely back at the Southern Sea Otter Sanctuary and Education Center.

When Logan and Ben arrived, Otter 1 was paddling around in her tank, looking like she hadn't left. You'd never know she was flipped out of a boat, was tossed around in a storm, and spent the night in the open ocean, completely vulnerable and helpless.

When they got to level 2, it was obvious Amy wanted to rush right in and see Otter 1, but Gina's tractor-beam gaze directed her to her office, where Amy sat down meekly. Gina shut the door. Gina liked Amy, but she didn't suffer fools gladly when it came to otters. The girl would have to say all the right things in order to get anywhere near her otters again.

Logan wisely stayed in the lab, talking with Ben, showing him where she and Bonnie found Solange. She didn't go down to the lower level, even though a crime-scene cleaner had thoroughly scoured away the blood. It still made her feel queasy.

Logan hoped Gina would be so relieved to have Otter 1 back, miraculously still in one piece, that she wouldn't spend a lot of energy being angry with Amy. Since Amy had more than paid for her bad choices by almost dying herself trying to escape a murderer, Logan also hoped Gina would let Amy back in as a volunteer. She could have left Otter 1's carrier behind but had tried to save her by taking her with her on the boat into the storm. That counted for something.

Twenty minutes later, when Gina emerged from her office, a much-chastised, but relieved Amy followed behind.

Logan let out a breath. Ben stood behind her, and Amy and Liam pulled up stools.

"Okay, team," Gina announced, "a lot has happened in the last forty-eight hours. Just so you know, until Solange is able to communicate and tells me otherwise, I am going to continue to do what she hired me to do: get this Southern Sea Otter Sanctuary and Education Center up and running by August 28, for the grand opening. I have no news as to the status of the lawsuit with her half brother. No news is good news, as far as I'm concerned.

"Jeff's death is tragic, and I just don't know what to say about the man who killed him and attacked you, Amy, other than I hope they catch him soon. No news on that, as far as I know. I presume they are working very hard on finding his killer."

No one had anything to add. They all felt the loss of this young man's life.

"As far as Otter 1. Physically, she's stable. Amy, your feeding her just before you went out probably saved her life. She was able to survive through the night, until someone found her."

Amy looked incredibly grateful for the bone Gina tossed her.

"But we won't know about the bonding problem until we work with her again, particularly you, Amy. We've got a four-year-old female otter coming up from La Jolla. The one Dennis and I went down to see. We're picking her up tomorrow. She's been in quarantine, but is healthy enough to transfer. She may or may not be a good surrogate mother for Otter 1. Looks like she's had at least one pup already. We'll just have to see how things go."

She looked around the room at her trained and semitrained volunteers.

Without mentioning Jeff's death again, Gina announced, "We're going to have to make a new schedule. Everyone in?"

Everyone was.

38

Detective Anderson looked at his watch. Looked at his inbox. Ignored his inbox. Lacing his fingers, he stretched out his arms and cracked his knuckles.

He hated waiting. What little forensic evidence there was from the crime scene was being worked on. Slim to zero chance of anything there. They'd call if they found anything. Not much more he could do.

He already interviewed the McKenna girl, the only witness who could still talk. She tried to be helpful but hadn't been able to tell him much.

"Big, tall, scary guy with a strong grip, wearing a suit and a welder's mask" was not exactly a precise description.

Esturban swabbed the inside of the mask they found on the floor in the lab, which had plenty of organic material. They'd run it, but he wasn't expecting much. It was secure in the evidence locker until they could put some more pieces together.

The only other thing they had were some fingerprints on the stainless steel lab table. All the other prints had been matched to the director, her assistant, the McKenna woman and her daughter, and the other volunteers and a delivery guy. And of course, the woman who almost got killed.

Until that woman, Solange something—he never could pronounce her last name—came to, he had no one else to talk to and no other leads to track down.

The McKenna girl didn't see his face, but maybe the older woman did. Maybe the guy's mask slipped, or she saw him before or after he put it on. No one knew which of the women, or the kid he killed, was attacked first. Solange was still in the hospital, unable to communicate, and the only other witness was dead. Poor kid.

The security cameras would have captured it all, but although installed, the ones in the lab were never set up. The director, Gina, thought they had been live, but only the ones outside had been activated. Her assistant, Dennis, felt bad about that. He'd been meaning to, but things were busy, etc., etc. . . .

Excuses are like assholes, buddy. We all have one, and they all stink.

Being a nice guy, he hadn't said that out loud, but he wanted to. He wished he'd given his own son more advice like that— talked more honestly to him, told him like it was—but his wife always made him back off, said he was too hard on the boy. Well, if he had been allowed to speak in his own house to his own son, maybe . . .

With great effort, Detective Andrews pulled his mind back to the closet he called his office. It was always dark in here. Some genius on the council decided every city office should turn off half their lights to save on electricity. Better for the environment, too, they said.

Grabbing his suit coat from the back of his chair, in two

long strides, he was at the door. Pausing, he reached over and flipped both light switches firmly up before exiting.

Luckily, Jasper's police station was a small one. Forensics was just down the hall. One small office, two desks. Tight fit. Esturban and the new guy shared. Esturban was supposed to be training him, but it was more like the other way around.

"What a surprise," Ken said, looking up from his Double-Double with extra cheese, not looking surprised at all.

Baby faced, with straight sandy hair and brown eyes, forty-two-year-old new-hire Ken Willet could handle most any forensic task, but was particularly gifted with fingerprints. The chief normally wouldn't have the funds to get someone as skilled or experienced as Ken, but thanks to a confluence of personal and professional events in the man's life, he had moved as far away from Saginaw, Michigan, as possible. Claimed to hate the snow. No one asked, and he didn't tell. Anderson was just glad he was here. He'd helped clear a couple of tough cases already.

Good man. *And* he worked Sundays. Apparently, neither one of them had a personal life. Esturban, a mostly happily married father of three, did not work weekends if he could help it.

Looking up from a desk covered with stacks of papers, file folders, Post-it notes, and unidentified former food items, Ken wiped some ketchup off the corner of his mouth. "Didn't I see your ugly mug in here just a few minutes ago?"

"A few hours ago."

Arms folded, Detective Anderson leaned against the row of filing cabinets lining the opposite wall. No way he was going to enter the room. Not without a hazmat suit.

"Got anything for me?" he asked.

Ken swallowed the last of his In-N-Out burger, balled up

the wrapper, and made a basket in the trashcan by the door. The can was half-full already, and the surrounding floor was clear. Impressive.

"Two points!"

"And to think the Lakers let you go . . . ," Anderson observed.

Unfazed by the detective's remark, Ken found one last fry that had escaped and popped it into his mouth before wiping his fingers on his pants and refreshing his computer screen with a tap.

"How do you find anything in that mess?" Anderson couldn't help but ask.

"Ahh . . . just be glad I can, Detective, just be glad I can," Ken said, rapidly scrolling through the screen in front of him. He turned it toward the door and motioned Andrews over to take a look.

"Here he is," Ken said, looking up at Andrews. "Your guy is Gary, Gary Schofield, California attorney at law. Address, phone—all there. Do you want me to forward it to you?"

"Yeah," Andrews said, taking out his notebook, jotting down the information manually. He didn't trust computers.

"Why didn't his name come up the first time?" he asked.

"Jeesh . . . ! Show a little gratitude," Ken said, but continued. "The first run only catches bad guys—it searches the criminal databases. I had to go back and run it through the state systems. Everybody who works for the state, is licensed by the state, has to be fingerprinted. Teachers, day-care workers, prison guards, attorneys . . . hmm . . . I see a theme here . . ." Ken reached behind him, catching a couple pieces of paper being spit out by the printer. "Here you go," he said, popping the pages into a surprisingly clean manila file folder he retrieved from the morass on his desk, handing it to him.

Ignoring him, Andrews took the folder and tapped the edge

on the door frame by way of acknowledgment. "Got it," he said, turning to lope back to his office.

Finally, he had something to work on. He was halfway down the hall before Ken's voice reached him.

"You're welcome!"

What does he want, flowers?

39

SUNDAY, JULY 26, 2015

After a seven-hour flight seated next to a woman on her way to Machu Picchu "to finally do something for *myself*, take care of *me* for a change . . . ," the Guadalajara terminal looked like heaven. Gary couldn't wait to get off that plane.

Even though he hadn't done more than nod and grunt in response to the recently divorced fiftysomething's self-help ramblings, it hadn't stopped her from telling him how her new therapist had helped her "*totally* let go" and forgive that *bastard*, her ex-husband, whose faults she then proceeded to list. In detail.

As the captain came on the air, asking everyone to buckle their seat belts and prepare for landing, she began sharing numerous quotes from the Dalai Lama. Had he read his book, *The Art of Happiness*?

Gary hadn't.

He hadn't checked any luggage, either, so when the flight attendant finally released them, he followed the rest of the sheeple off the plane, grateful she couldn't corner him in baggage claim.

Happiness was more than Gary hoped for. But he did want to live.

Exiting the terminal was a shock. Walking into the hot, wet air was like pushing through a thick blanket. The cancer treatment center would have air conditioning. He hoped. From the pictures online, the grounds were immaculate and the whole facility gleamed modern and clean. He just had to get there.

He got the first cab in line and directed him to Oasis de Milagro. The driver seemed familiar with this address. A lot of Americans must come down here for treatments not approved in the States.

Gary leaned back into the seat and closed his eyes against the pain. It was almost unbearable now, but he made it. He was here. Now all he had to do was give Oasis de Milagro the initial payment and get this treatment started. There was nothing left for him to do but place himself in the hands of these cutting-edge doctors. If anyone could beat this cancer, Gary hoped it was them. Each doctor on staff came with long lists of diplomas from places like Johns Hopkins and the Mayo Clinic. Each had done excellent research and won awards in their fields. He would be in good hands.

Right now, though, all he wanted was drugs. He'd held off on the pain meds in order to think clearly enough to get here. The nurse he spoke to on the phone just before leaving promised they would relieve his pain and symptoms within twenty-four hours of arrival.

Once he was thinking clearly, he would call Felix and hit him and Bill up for the cash he needed for the second half of his treatment. The Oasis de Milagro was a miracle all right—a miracle anyone could afford it. He needed that money.

Why did that French woman have to be so stubborn? But

it would be okay. He had Bill and Felix still. Plan B. One of them would buy the rights, he was sure of it. His driver threaded the car confidently through incomprehensible traffic, so Gary allowed himself to learn back against the seat and rest his eyes.

Twenty minutes later, Gary was awakened by the sudden cessation of the taxi's rumbling, spitting engine. He reached for his briefcase and momentarily panicked before finding it on the floor at his feet. Must have slipped during the ride. Letting out a small sigh of relief, he clutched the handle firmly in one hand and got out of the cab.

He hadn't converted his money yet, but the driver seemed happy to accept dollars, so he thrust what he hoped was close to the correct amount at him through the open window and looked around to find the front entrance. There must be some mistake. He turned back to the driver.

"Oasis de Milagro?" he asked.

"*Si*, Oasis de Milagro!" the driver called back as he pulled away from the curb, pointing to a small metal sign a few feet away.

Gary stared at the two-story cinderblock building squatting in front of him. Traffic continued to whizz behind him along the very busy street. A row of small windows, all but one of them closed, topped a single door propped open with a rock.

Frantically searching for any signs of similarity between this prison block and the luxurious resort-style facility he saw on the clinic's website, Gary turned left to walk around the building. Maybe it looked better from the other side. A spindly row of anemic palm trees was all that was left of the full tropical landscaping in the site's pictures, but unfortunately, it did look like the right place, just the wrong decade—or maybe century. Whatever Oasis de Milagro used to be, it wasn't anymore.

He couldn't just turn around and go back to the States.

The French woman and the boy were both dead. The girl had escaped. She never saw his face, but he couldn't risk the police being smarter than they were on TV shows and identifying him through some new CSI technology. No, going home wasn't an option.

He was exhausted. The pain was so much worse than before, and he could barely see out of his right eye. For now, he had no other choice but to walk in. He needed a place to regroup. He hoped the doctors at least were as advertised, even if the facility was woefully not.

Hunching his shoulders, tightening his grip on his briefcase, he strode toward the entrance. He refused to walk through any door held open with a rock.

40

Felix disconnected the call, then slammed the file drawer shut with his foot.

That son of a bitch.

He'd been working at home when Gary called. Attorneys were supposed to fix problems like this, not create them.

"You okay, hon?" his wife called from the kitchen.

"Everything's fine," he said, getting up to close the door.

She knew better than to bother him in here. She didn't need to hear any of this. He kept his business and his home life strictly separated.

A minute later, his cell vibrated. He looked at the screen. If it was Gary again, he could leave a message. He wasn't in the mood to talk. Not until he calmed down.

Bill.

That didn't take long. Felix closed his eyes. Gary must have called him next. He didn't want to pick up. He needed time to think. But if he didn't answer, Bill would keep calling. He was probably in panic mode. Reluctantly, Felix tapped the answer icon and put in his Bluetooth earpiece.

"Bill," he said.

As predicted, Bill was freaking out. "Did you know about this?"

"Of course not. It's Gary's job to find any wrinkles like this and smooth them over. Unfortunately, he's a little too good at his job and only smoothed things over for himself," Felix said.

Once he talked Bill away from the ledge, he could get off the phone and think this through. There was always a solution. He just needed to think. And if Bill would ever shut up, he could.

"I'm going to have to tell Labovitch," Bill said. "I can't believe how screwed up this is!"

"Look," Felix added, "it's going to be fine. Hold off for a few days."

Bill's next few words were dripping in sarcasm. "I can't 'hold off for a few days,' Felix! My company—on my recommendation—is filing for permits this week. Labovitch trusts me. When he finds out that not only is the land now occupied by a center for cute little sea otters, it's in the middle of an unresolved title dispute, *and* that big pool of oil under it belongs to someone else . . . let's just say that will not go well for me."

Felix knew Bill's main concern was padding his escape fund so he could leave his wife and sail away with that airhead he'd been seeing.

Bill continued, "When they find out someone else owns the mineral rights . . . and that someone is an attorney who knows what they're worth, I'll be lucky if all I lose is my job. Labovitch isn't stupid. As long as everything is going smoothly, he's happy to pretend I am just a lucky guesser, but the minute there's a problem, he'll happily throw me under the bus. Just for spite."

Felix listened. Bill's unspoken threat was loud and clear. If he went down, he'd take Felix down with him. Using thumper trucks in residential areas on land that didn't belong to you was illegal nine ways to Sunday. If Bill fell apart, Felix knew he would have no compunction about dragging him down with him. And if Bill spilled his guts, Scott would find out and he'd lose both deals.

Bill's harangue was winding down. "I held up my part of the bargain, now you need to hold up yours. This guy is your screwup, your attorney, not mine. Fix this, Felix!"

How dare Bill threaten him. He'd taken all the risks. He'd hired the thumper trucks and the men to do the unauthorized surveys on private land. Bill had made a bundle on those unofficial reports. What was he complaining about?

Bill's voice rose in anxiety. "You've got to fix this!"

Spineless jellyfish.

Felix could just picture the little weasel, sweating bullets in his big office overlooking the bay. He wanted to hang up on the little twit, but he couldn't let him spiral out of control. He sighed. "Already on it, Bill. Nothing for you to worry about." Felix leaned back in his chair, almost believing his own words. "I've got it handled."

"Well," said Bill, slightly mollified, "you'd better."

I really hate this guy.

"Call you tomorrow," Felix said.

With that, they hung up. Felix grabbed his keys and told Celia he was going in to the office for a while.

He did his best thinking in the car.

By the time he pulled into his parking spot, Felix had a huge smile on his face. He had the perfect solution to this problem . . . and Gary wasn't going to like it.

For that matter, neither would Bill.

Gary thought he was safe in Guadalajara, but Felix had cousins in Guadalajara. Cousins who wouldn't mind if there was one less gringo in the world. He knew one who might even do the job for free.

41

Diaz found a space near the elevators in short-term parking. If all went well, they'd be back tonight. Andrews was halfway across the lot before his partner clicked the lock shut. They had thirty minutes to spare.

All they had were the fingerprints, and the McKenna girl's description of her attacker, which fit the approximate height and weight on the attorney's driver's license. Not a lot to go on, but somehow, his lieutenant had managed to push a search warrant through.

They needn't have rushed. Due to overbooking by the airlines, they cooled their heels at the terminal. They finally caught a Southwest flight into Oakland at 3:00 p.m. The only rental car selection left was a Chrysler Sebring convertible.

"Sweet!" his partner said.

Andrews was not thrilled. It probably only got two miles to the gallon. In his opinion, driving was for getting from point A to point B. Period.

They were on the road just in time for rush-hour traffic. Diaz insisted on driving with the top down.

By the time they pulled into the driveway of 2198 Hamilton Way, Andrews's mood had not improved. His butt was sore, his back was sore, and the last thing he had to eat was a bagel at the airport. He also didn't have a hat, so he'd spent the last twenty-six miles having his neatly combed hair blasted into an infinite number of punk-rock hairdos. It was coated in road grime. Attempting to finger comb it out of his eyes was not entirely successful.

"Perfect," he mumbled.

Diaz ignored him.

Andrews slammed the car door shut a little harder than necessary. The heat was stark and oppressive. The Inland Empire had nothing on Oakland. Must be ninety in the shade.

He straightened his tie. This was probably a wild-goose chase, but it was the only lead they had. Playing devil's advocate in his mind, Andrews knew the guy could have been at that center for any reason—maybe he loved sea otters and wanted to make a donation.

Might as well get this over with. Even with the delays, they were still well within the 6:00 a.m. to 10:00 p.m. allowable time frame for the warrant.

When knocking on the door yielded no response, they let themselves in. The fingerprints and description gave them enough to arrest, if not hold, Schofield, should they find him on the premises, but after committing murder, Andrews didn't expect him to stick around and answer questions.

All they could hope for was to find something to point them in the right direction, anything indicating where he'd gone or why an attorney from Northern California would want to kill a kid and attempt to kill an old woman.

DEVIL'S CLAW

The judge gave them unusually wide search parameters for the residence, including the garage. The car was look but don't touch, if it happened to be there, which it wasn't. That's the first thing they'd checked when they got inside. People kept all kinds of things in their cars. And presumably, he drove himself in his own car to the center. They were still checking ride shares, but no taxis had picked up or dropped off anyone at that location.

Andrews ducked back inside the house started pulling on plastic booties and gloves. Probably not necessary, but still. They didn't know what they had yet. No dead body, but you never knew. They hadn't checked the freezer yet.

Andrews was hoping they'd get lucky. The guy hadn't been all that careful at the sea otter center, so he probably didn't cover his tracks here, either. They'd find something.

The kitchen and dining area yielded nothing other than the fact that Schofield didn't cook and barely ate at home. Full set of china neatly stacked in the cupboards. No dirty dishes. Not even a box of cereal in the shallow pantry next to the stove. The only thing in the fridge was a stick of butter, some condiments, and takeout containers.

Man ate well, though. Steak, green beans, and half a baked potato in one Styrofoam box. Mostly dried out. Lid popped open. Shriveled cheesecake. No alcohol. Not even beer.

"Maybe he doesn't like to drink alone," Diaz said, materializing at his shoulder.

"Eats out mostly, that's for sure," Andrews said, forcing himself not to flinch. The guy was a ninja.

They tossed the couch, checked all the usual hiding places behind the TV and in the vents, undid the remote control, poked around the baseboards, then headed upstairs.

In the first bedroom, they took in the open suitcase and clothing on the bed and floor. Diaz raised his eyebrows.

"Interrupted packing for a trip?"

Andrews shrugged. They conducted a thorough search but found no laptops, ticket stubs, or pads of paper on the nightstand with conveniently remaining impressions of airline reservations or secret rendezvous on them.

A quick search of the closet and dresser didn't yield anything more.

What did yield something useful was in the second bedroom. Eight-by-seven feet, it wasn't much bigger than a walk-in closet. Schofield's home office.

"Bingo," said Diaz. "Now we're talkin'."

A older desktop computer topped a small but solid wood desk. Another table ran along the wall under the window, creating an L-shaped work area. At the far end, a bulky printer/copier/fax machine connected to a landline.

"Our guy's old-school," Andrews said.

Going by the interrupted packing and seemingly quick exit, it was doubtful Schofield took the time to wipe the computer clean. But even if he'd done that before packing, between Ken and Esturban, whatever secrets the attorney hid in that archaic box of bits and bytes would be printed and on his desk by tomorrow morning.

All he had to do was pack it up and get it to them tonight. Conveniently, Schofield kept the original packaging on a shelf in the closet.

Feeling like they were finally getting somewhere, Andrews didn't even object when Diaz put on a rap station on the way to the airport.

It was late when he got the report, but Ken came through. Detective Andrews now knew more about Schofield than his mother. It always amazed him how much information you could learn about someone from their computer. People blithely conducted their private lives online and over the phone, even the ones who should know better, like an attorney. Which reminded him, he'd have to change all of his passwords when he got home.

He had it all. Bank accounts. Doctor's reports. Phone calls. E-mails. Browsing history. Ken did his usual great job. But he had gone above and beyond official job duties on this one. Ken really wanted to nail this guy. A few minutes ago, he came into Andrews's office and handed him a folded piece of paper, exiting without saying anything.

Oasis de Milagro, Guadalajara.

Andrews looked it up on his computer. It was one of those cancer treatment centers.

Ken, you are my new best friend. Maybe he'd send him flowers after all.

Within minutes, Andrews was in his car. He drove a few miles inland to a RadioShack and picked up a burner phone, then punched in the number of a retired cop he knew.

International call.

He looked at his watch. 8:30 p.m. Two hours later there. Sheila was one of those "early to bed, early to rise" types, but if she didn't pick up, he'd leave a message. After getting her leg shot up in a gang takedown, she got out with a medical. Last he heard, she'd been enjoying the good life in Manzanillo. He hoped she'd help him out. Once a cop, always a cop.

He checked Google Maps. It was only a three-hour drive to Guadalajara. All he needed her to do was locate Schofield for him; then they'd work on extradition.

Sheila picked up on the second ring. Living on Mexico time, she said, when he asked. No need to get up early anymore. They exchanged a few pleasantries; then he explained why he had called.

"Most of the cops down here are bent," she said, "but I know a few we might not have to bribe . . . much."

With promises to call as soon as she located his guy, they hung up. With nothing else to do, he dug some sweats out of a pile of dirty clothes and decided to take a run. For someone who hated waiting, he'd gotten into a job that required a lot of it.

Andrews lived just a few blocks from the ocean but couldn't remember the last time he'd run on the beach. It was louder than he remembered. A stiff breeze cooled his face and made his eyes water momentarily. This was definitely what he needed. He needed to clear his mind and sweat the day away.

In about a mile, he was slightly winded and turned back. He really needed to get back in shape. He promised himself to start a workout schedule tomorrow.

Except for the moon and a pair of lovers on a blanket up by the rocks, he had the sand to himself. When he was coming up on Main Beach, he spotted another runner pounding the sand, coming toward him. A silhouette of long legs, topped by a formfitting T-shirt got his attention. Nice . . . When she got closer, he recognized the runner as the McKenna woman. Logan.

If she recognized him, she didn't acknowledge it.

She passed him in a flash. Didn't look winded at all. He looked back to watch her run. She'd pulled her hair into a thick braid. It glinted copper in the moonlight.

Thoughts of unbraiding that hair and wrapping those long limbs around him froze him momentarily to the spot. He watched her run away from him until a cloud covered the moon, making it too dark to see.

42

MONDAY, JULY 27, 2015

"**C**ome in, Mr. Schofield! Please come in and have a seat," the doctor said, standing up from behind a solid, heavy wooden desk, waving Gary into his office. Dr. Manning, according to the name tag on his white coat, indicated a chair across from his desk, reached across, and held out his hand, forcing Gary to shake it.

"Welcome to Oasis de Milagro!" he said, sitting back down.

A large man with thick, wavy brown hair and ruddy cheeks, Manning looked well fed and self-satisfied. Coal-black eyes emanated a confident energy into the room.

Gary did as requested, but from what he'd seen so far, he severely doubted that any kind of miracles would be worked here. Still, the room had been clean, the bed adequate, and the staff certainly attentive. And whatever they'd given him last night certainly worked better than the pain meds he'd received in the US. He held out a sliver of hope.

"I trust you rested well last night. Our first goal is to make you as comfortable as possible. There is no reason for any of our guests to be in pain. Have you had breakfast?"

"No, I wasn't hungry," Gary said. He had no appetite this morning, but the drugs had indeed knocked him out last night. He had enjoyed the first solid night's sleep he'd had in a long time. If that was the price of being pain-free, he didn't much care.

"Well, maybe you'll have some lunch. You can always get something sent up from the kitchen even if you don't feel hungry. You need to keep your strength up. You are free to eat anything you want. No dietary restrictions here. In fact, your treatments will work better with food on your stomach."

That was certainly different. Made it feel more like a resort than a hospital.

Gary noticed the doctor had no accent. He sounded as American as he was. He looked at the wall behind him where his diplomas were displayed.

The doctor noticed him looking.

"Medical school in Chicago, residency in LA," he said. "Received an excellent education in the US, but as I'm sure you read on the website, our hands are tied there. When it comes to treating cancer, anyway. Any good oncologist knows this is where you go to be at the cutting edge. Mexico is one of the few places we are free to practice real medicine. I started this clinic about eight years ago, and we have helped many, many people, with cases more advanced than yours, Gary."

Gary preferred Mr. Schofield, but the residual drugs in his system kept him from objecting.

"The *doctors* are in charge here, not the insurance companies or the FDA," the doctor added in a more aggressive tone. "We have access to many more advanced therapies here." He quickly shifted back to cheerful and optimistic, getting down to business. "Allow me to introduce you to my colleague Dr. Rolphson," he said, indicating a man who had just entered the room. "He is one of the highly skilled members of the medical team dedicated to your care."

The small, thin man, also replete in white doctor's coat with name tag, remained standing after leaning forward to shake Gary's hand.

"Today we want you to rest from your journey and get the lay of the land, so to speak. Nurse Gonzalez will show you where everything is. We have a very nice patio area for dining, should you prefer not to take meals in your room. I do encourage you to eat something, but first, as you know, unlike American medical facilities, we receive no funds from insurance companies or the government. Nurse Gonzalez will take you to see Miss Monroe two doors down. She will take care of your payment now so you will be free to focus on your treatment tomorrow."

Nurse Gonzalez appeared at the door and smoothly ushered him down the hall toward the efficient Miss Monroe.

As soon as they left, Drs. Manning and Rolphson took another look at Gary's imaging results.

"Nothing we can do for him, you know," Rolphson said.

"Of course not, but he doesn't know that. He's got a few weeks left, but who knows, he could last months."

Dr. Rolphson looked uncomfortable. He'd only been here a few months.

"Don't let it get to you, Rolphson," Dr. Manning said. "There's nothing wrong with giving these people hope and making them more comfortable before they die. Yes, we make a ton of money, but they are going to die anyway, and at least we can drug them to the hilt until then."

Dr. Rolphson still looked doubtful.

"Would you rather go back the States and deal with insurance companies?"

7:43 p.m.

After making the initial payment, which bought him a couple of months of unlimited treatment and residency at the center, Gary's funds were all but depleted. Thanks to the unplanned events at the sea otter center, he hadn't been able to sell his new Lincoln before he flew out, but as soon as he made his phone calls in the morning, he'd have plenty of cash. Felix would be angry, he knew, but he was also a pragmatic man. He'd fork over the money to get the mineral rights. He would know how to leverage that into more money than he would pay to Gary.

He would make the phone calls now, but just getting here, making the payment, and following Nurse Gonzalez around on her extensive tour had exhausted him. She gently insisted he eat dinner, which she assured him was delicious. Some kind of Mexican goop. It looked okay, but he couldn't smell or taste much, so he only forced about half of it down. Nurse Gonzalez stopped in to give him his nightly medicine and make sure he was settled in for the evening. He docilely allowed himself to be hooked up to the IV, and the lovely medicine began dripping in.

She dimmed the lights but didn't turn them out completely. He requested the window be left open. No air conditioning, but he was surprised how little it bothered him.

"Okay, Mr. Schofield, are you comfortable?"

Gary was already starting to fade. He felt marvelous.

"I'm going home now, but if you need anything, just push the red call button on the wall above your bed, on your right."

DEVIL'S CLAW

Already drifting toward happy land, Gary did not respond.

Nurse Gonzalez smiled. They only kept one night nurse on duty for seventeen patients. No one ever woke up at night.

43

TUESDAY, JULY 28, 2015, 12:33 A.M.

Eduardo checked his money belt one more time. He'd learned not to carry anything you didn't want ripped off your shoulder. Or leave anything of value in your room.

Everything was good to go. It hadn't taken long to get what he needed. One thing about Mexico, you could go into any *farmacias* and buy things over the counter you had to jump through hoops for back home.

Even then, for what he wanted, you normally had to get a prescription from a Mexican doctor and purchase it at a *primera clase*. But like everything else in Guadalajara, you could get anything for a price.

Zipping up the belt, he made sure his shirt covered it before he let himself out into the street. People were still enjoying the warm summer night. He started walking. Julio would be parked around the corner.

Eduardo still didn't feel at home here, but he'd quickly learned how to get around. He had to, just to survive.

Twenty-eight years ago, when he was just a toddler, his parents carried him across the border. They made it to Gilroy, where relatives took them in and got them work picking strawberries. They never looked back.

In college, he met and married Vanessa. They were both working on their nursing degrees when he got picked up on a DUI after a friend's bachelor party.

That was seven months ago. That's when his life changed. The only country he'd ever known deported his ass back to Mexico, his "home" country. He'd never been to Mexico and only spoke rudimentary Spanish. His parents had insisted he speak English, anxious for him to fit in.

Vanessa, six months pregnant, desperate to get him back, sold his car and hired an immigration attorney that said he specialized in cases like his. But after the guy got paid, he either ignored Vanessa's calls or asked for more money. He wanted more money than either of them had or could borrow to get him back home again. And he had to get home.

Here he lived in constant fear and hunger. He couldn't speak the language. He had no job. Vanessa sent money, but half the time, it didn't get through. And now that they'd given that bloodsucking attorney everything they had, she had no more money to send.

Last week, she contacted her cousin Felix Rodriguez. Vanessa didn't know him well, but he was known in the family for getting things done.

So when Felix called, Eduardo listened. Even though he listened with growing alarm as Felix described what he wanted him to do, what he tried to focus on was the golden passport that would get him back home. Back home to his family, his country, his life—and a wife about to deliver his second child. Felix said it came with a rock-solid social security number, too. Vanessa would never have to worry again.

The fact that the slime he wanted to get rid of was an attorney helped Eduardo say yes. He could do this. Well, he may not have the stomach to do it himself, but he knew someone who did.

If all went well, he'd be back home with Vanessa in time for the birth of his new daughter.

Julio was there. Waiting until Eduardo got in, he said nothing, but drove at a steady pace toward the Oasis de Milagro clinic. Julio knew the way. Eduardo didn't know his last name and didn't need to. After tonight, hopefully, he'd never see Julio or anyone else in this godforsaken rat hole again.

1:16 a.m.

The streets were quiet. Oasis de Milagro sat sleepily in the middle of the block. If they had a security system, it wasn't in evidence. The two men walked quickly around to the back side of the property, by some scraggly palms. Several of the windows were open. They selected the one farthest from what looked like the well-lit nurse's station in the center and hoisted themselves easily up and in. Once inside, they listened, but all they heard was the person softly snoring in the bed. He hadn't moved a muscle, but still, after making sure the coast was clear, they stepped softly into the hall.

Felix had provided a description of Gary Schofield. An over-six-foot-tall man with wiry hair and a beak-like nose wasn't hard to find. They found him in room 216, sound asleep like everyone else on the floor. No breeze came through the open window. Eduardo would not miss the heat.

Indicating silently that Julio should provide lookout by the door, Eduardo stepped quickly to the far side of the bed, unzipping his money belt and removing a small vial as he went.

He just wanted to get this over with. With only a moment's

hesitation, he added the contents of the vial to Gary's IV. He had come prepared with a syringe just in case, but this was better. No needle mark.

This wasn't how he'd planned on using his nursing knowledge, but he had no choice. He would just have to live with what he had done when he got back home.

Gary's eyes fluttered open, but he did not move.

"Mr. Schofield. Don't try to move. You won't be able to."

Gary's eyes widened in panic.

"Felix told me what you did. You killed that poor boy. You deserve to die, that's not a question. And what you stole will be returned to Felix. I'll see to that."

Eduardo reattached Gary's IV to the original drip and placed the vial he had brought back into his money belt.

The fear and desperation in Gary's eyes would have softened his heart seven months ago—a lifetime ago. Now, it only made him hurry. Locating the briefcase, he easily found the paper Felix had described, folded and tucked it inside the second pocket of the money belt, then waved Julio over.

"Sorry, Gary, but my medical expertise is limited—I'm not sure I gave you enough. Julio is here to finish the job."

He had no qualms about killing Gary. He just couldn't do this part himself. Just before he let himself out of the window to the grounds outside, Eduardo saw the glint of the knife and the sick smile on Julio's face as he approached Gary's bed.

44

"Mr. Schofield?"

Making her last rounds before the end of her shift, the short, middle-aged night nurse waited a minute before knocking again. It was still early. Sometimes the patients slept a lot during their treatments.

Still, his sister had come a long way. The regular nurses didn't arrive until 8:00 a.m. She was just a nurse's aide, really, only authorized to call one of them if there was an emergency between midnight and 8:00 a.m.

She knocked again, a little louder this time, opening the door slowly as she did so.

"Mr. Schofield, your sister is here to visit you. I'm just going to turn the light on now. Be sure to close your eyes if the light bothers you . . ."

The first thing she saw was the wide-open window and the contents of his briefcase dumped on a small chair. Some items had spilled out and fallen to the floor. A familiar odor assaulted her senses. Mr. Schofield must have had an accident. It happened. It wasn't pleasant, but she could deal with that.

But there was another smell, too. Vaguely metallic. She turned toward the bed.

Madre de Dios!

Stifling a scream, the woman crossed herself; then, trying not to step into the thick puddle of drying blood by the bed, she reached past the dead man's ruined face and hit the red call button.

Help summoned, she then hurried out to comfort his sister and keep her from going into that room.

45

In a town whose population doubled every summer, except among the locals, the deaths of Mrs. Houser and Jeff Larson barely made a ripple. After the storm that blew through, summer returned to Southern California perfect, in the seventies to eighties every day. Mild breezes, cranberry sunsets. Tourists filled the sidewalks, restaurants were humming, and families set up coolers and umbrellas on the beach.

This morning, they were on their way to Jeff's memorial service. Lowering the window on Ben's truck to get some fresh air, Logan felt disconnected. All she saw were strangers. She loved Jasper best in the winter, when she knew most of the people she saw on the sidewalks. During the summer, every square inch seemed to be crowded with tourists who thought Jasper existed just to entertain them a few days or weeks out of every year.

Still, she enjoyed the familiar sounds and smells of summer. Brought back memories of growing up here. Suntan oil, caramel apples, briny seaweed, all drifted in the window on waves of cumbia, hip-hop, and oldies as they drove past Main Beach.

She thought of the conversation she'd had with Amy this morning. Over a couple of cups of coffee—Liam made great coffee and left a fresh pot before heading out early to help Amosa with the kelp beds—it didn't take long for Amy's feelings to bubble up and over, coming out with tears and a flood of unanswerable questions.

"Why didn't I realize what was going on?" Amy said. "I've been so wrapped up in Sadie and in love with Liam, I was completely oblivious to Jeff's feelings. He would not have been at the center if it hadn't been for me." She paused to get a grip on herself. "It's my fault, Mom! If he didn't bring that stuff for me, he wouldn't have been there. He wouldn't be . . . he wouldn't be dead . . . ," she said, sobbing into her napkin.

Logan understood. She was still trying to wrap her own head around Jeff's death. He was one of the gentlest, kindest, and most talented young people she knew. Jeff's death was a tragedy in every sense of the word.

Helpless in the face of her daughter's raw pain, Logan reached across and grabbed one of her hands. She was not going to let her daughter dissolve into an endless morass of guilt.

Amy grieved when her father died, but this was different. This wasn't just grief; it was also guilt. Oversized guilt. So much had happened. Malaria, then her harrowing escape from a murderer, followed by losing Sadie, and almost losing her own life during that summer storm at sea.

When Amy's tears slowed to sniffles, Logan squeezed her hands. No matter how she felt herself, it was her job to be the grown-up. Her job to comfort her daughter.

"Honey, look at me," Logan said.

Amy, snuffling, gave her mother a hopeless look.

"This is not your fault. Boys get crushes, and yes, he was there, but not just to bring your things. He brought his own laundry back, too. You are not responsible for his being attacked. That man—whoever attacked Solange and killed Jeff—*he* is responsible, not you. I wish I could make life nice and neat for you, honey," Logan said, "but the truth is life is messy. We just have to learn to live with things we can't change. You're a good person. You need to remember that."

The principal was organizing this memorial to help the students deal with the unexpected death of a young friend. Even though school was out for the summer, most students were local. A large turnout was expected. Amy and Liam were already there, saving them seats.

Ben parked and Logan brought herself back to the present. They walked inside, found Amy and Liam, and took their seats.

The principal did a good job, Logan thought. After welcoming everyone, he highlighted Jeff's character as well as his talent, focusing on the importance of taking advantage of every moment we have, developing the gifts we've been given, overcoming our weaknesses, to make the world a better place. They played one of the songs from the fund-raising album, then turned the time over for anyone who knew Jeff to come up and share their thoughts about him. Brandon, although he had to stop once to get control of himself, captured Jeff's personality best, including sharing a funny story about his best friend's first surfing lesson.

Logan left the public speaking to the students but went up after the service to give her personal condolences to the family.

Liam went with Ben to pull the car around. Logan stayed with Amy. She wanted a few minutes alone with her to make sure she was doing okay. They found a side gate open and sat at one of the lunch tables in the quad.

You couldn't hear the ocean from here; the only sound was an oriole warbling his heart out in a stand of eucalyptus trees that ran along the edge of the basketball court. A soft breeze scattered a few dry leaves across the blacktop.

Logan wasn't sure how to start the conversation, but she didn't have to worry. Amy started it for her.

"Mom, do you believe in heaven?" Amy asked. "I mean, we didn't go to church or anything, but . . ."

Logan thought about what to say. Personally, she had more questions than answers, but she didn't want to burst any spiritual bubbles Amy had, if they gave her comfort. She knew a lot of the service workers in Africa must be sponsored by churches. Maybe Amy had picked up some nascent religious beliefs. As always, though, Logan opted to tell her daughter the truth and respect her right to make up her own mind.

"I may not believe in God and hell and heaven in the traditional sense, but I think there's a balance. Light and dark, good and evil—I think somehow things are made right, although not always in the time or way we want or expect. Call it karma or whatever, but I think there are very real consequences to our actions, especially our intent. Jeff was a good person and did good things. Wherever or whatever heaven is, I'm sure he's smack dab in the middle of it. Probably playing his guitar."

Amy smiled.

"And that man," Logan added, ". . . that man, whoever he is, is responsible for his evil acts. He will not get away with this."

"I still feel bad, Mom," Amy said, rubbing a spot on the table with her finger.

Logan waited a minute before answering, not wanting to disregard her daughter's feelings, arranging her words carefully. "We all make mistakes, Amy, but your intent matters. You are the best human being I know—you'd never intend harm to anyone. That counts, Amy. You just have to believe that."

Amy nodded, drying her eyes before they walked to the front of the school, where Ben and Liam were waiting in the car. If not completely appeased, she was at least calmer and more relaxed. In time, Logan hoped, her daughter would accept her frailties and mistakes.

God knew Logan was still learning to accept hers.

46

SATURDAY, AUGUST 1, 2015

Released from intensive care several days ago, Solange was doing well and due to go home soon, according to Gina. Hopefully, she was up for a short visit. After dropping Amy and Liam off, Ben and Logan continued north past Jasper to Hoag Hospital.

"Hello, beautiful," Ben said, bending to kiss Solange's forehead, handing her a cheerful arrangement of yellow daisies and roses.

"Ahh, Ben! *Merci bien . . . très jolie!*"

Talking sounded painful. She barely spoke above a whisper.

A nurse followed them into the room, thoughtfully bringing a vase.

"Five minutes, guys. Her throat needs to rest. Don't let her do too much talking."

"*Bouffhh,*" Solange said, rolling her eyes and shrugging her shoulders in a typical French gesture.

Reaching up to hug Ben, kissing both his cheeks, she croaked, "I'm fine!"

Patting the bed next to her for Ben and indicating a chair for Logan to pull up.

"Logan," she said, looking directly into her eyes. "Thank you, and your friend . . . for . . ." She started coughing, and Ben got her a glass of water from her bedside table.

Logan demurred, saying truthfully that all they had done was call 911. She was just glad Solange was okay. She didn't mention Jeff's death. She wasn't sure if anyone had told Solange about it yet. Apparently, no one had, because she didn't seem to know anything about that or Amy being chased into the ocean with Otter 1, the storm, or any of the events after her attacker left her on the floor to die.

"I hear your daughter is engaged. It is Amy, correct? Please congratulate her for me . . . ," Solange said, taking another sip of water from the glass Ben had refilled.

Logan, happy to have a chance to end the visit on a lighter note, shared the engagement-announcement beach picnic, then acknowledged the nurse's time-to-leave signal at the door. Which was a good thing, because as much as she seemed to want to talk, Solange's voice was giving out.

Solange said Gina was planning on driving her home tomorrow when her doctor gave the final okay. Logan offered to give her a day to settle in; then she would bring dinner over. Monday, if that was okay with her.

Solange graciously accepted. Logan knew she could probably just order something in but was glad Solange allowed her to do this small thing. The tiny sculptress intimidated her, but in the few conversations they'd had over the last year, she discovered a person she'd like to get to know better.

The only dish Logan knew how to make was roast chicken

and a salad, but Ben promised to whip up something for sides and dessert before he left for work or give her something to take from his stockpile in the freezer. She hoped he'd make his fabulous flourless chocolate cake with raspberries on top. She loved that cake.

All Logan had to do was show up on Solange's doorstep Monday evening, food in hand. Solange said not to bother with wine, she had a late '90s bottle of Domaine aux Moines Savennieres from Roche aux Moines.

Of course she did.

Logan's mouth was already watering.

47

"Paper or plastic?"

Logan wondered how many times a day the cashier had to ask that question.

"Paper, please," Logan said.

She forgot again. Amy had given her three burlap, recyclable grocery totes with leather handles, but did she ever remember to take them out of the trunk? Noooo!

Back home, hoping she hadn't forgotten anything, Logan hauled the two bags onto her kitchen counter and started to unload. Chicken? Check. Butter? Check. Lemons? Where were the lemons?

Ben had planted some rosemary for her, which had turned into a bush on the side of the house, so she had plenty of that.

Just as she was putting the last of the salad makings into the fridge, her cell phone rang. She dug it out of her purse and put it on speaker while she folded the bags.

"Hello?"

A clear, commanding voice said, "Logan, glad you picked up. Rita Wolfe here."

"Rita." She quickly looked at the clock. Ten thirty. "Good morning, good to hear from you."

Why would Rita Wolfe, the principal of the New School up near Portland, Oregon, be calling her? She could still picture the wiry woman, the spitting image of Amelia Earhart if she'd survived to age gracefully.

She'd visited the New School last year while doing some research for Fractals. Friend and retired school nurse Glenda had invited her. Their computer instructor, Huey Le, had a sister whose mother-in-law had been killed in the explosion across the street from the hotel Logan had been staying at. She wondered how he and his sister were doing.

Rita got right to the point.

"Have an opening, Logan. Music and math. Think you'd be perfect for it," she said.

Logan didn't know what to say. She was flattered, of course. She admired Rita and everything she was doing at the New School.

Rita was creating just the kind of school Logan wished they had down here, but it was just an hour or so outside Portland. Oregon. A thousand miles away. From Ben. From Amy. From everything she was building here. She didn't know if Amy and Liam were going to stay or go back to Africa. They could move back to Scotland to be with Liam's family, for all Logan knew. You couldn't plan your life around your kids.

Taking a job at the New School would also mean leaving her new home. Not just the house she bought and fixed up, but the new life she'd forged for herself here. Friendships, Tava'e's. Where would she get her cinnamon rolls?

Besides, bless his heart, even though the funding for Fractals was up in the air, for now, Greuger hadn't pulled the plug. They were still exploring all other avenues for money while Mrs. Houser's family decided whether they were going to fulfill their recently deceased mother's financial commitments.

Jeff's death affected everyone in the Fractals family, teachers and students. The thought of going back into the recording studio without him seemed impossible. The program would come to a screeching halt if Mrs. Houser's family didn't come around or they couldn't find a new donor in the next few weeks. Salaries had to be paid, including hers, and the school district was refusing to put any money toward the program.

She'd exhausted all her financial resources buying and restoring her beach home and converting the garage to her office/studio for Fractals.

Maybe she should consider Rita's offer.

Being as honest and straight as Rita, Logan thanked her for her offer and explained her situation. If the funding for Fractals came through, she was staying put. If not, she would call her back and see if the job was still available.

As much as she hated to let go of the security of a backup job offer, it was the right thing to do. She took a deep breath and told Rita to keep looking so she could be fully staffed when school started in September. As much as she wanted to hedge her bets to make sure she had a job in the fall, she would just have to risk it.

Rita appreciated her honesty and told Logan to let her know if she changed her mind.

Logan put the folded bags in the recycling bin Amy and Liam had thoughtfully provided.

Why did life have to be so complicated? Just when things were starting to come together.

Logan looked around her tiny living room and took a deep breath. Nothing to do and nowhere to go right this minute. Ben was at work. She'd cleaned house early this morning to work off stress. Tomorrow she was meeting Bonnie to do some legwork on wedding venues for Amy. She didn't have to roast the chicken and take it over to Solange's until tomorrow afternoon/evening. She couldn't make any funding phone calls for Fractals until tomorrow morning.

Good. She needed some alone time, some total distraction. She walked over and retrieved her violin case. Nothing could drag her mind off the worry wheel and fill her with joy like music.

Her fingers itched to play, and Bella was happy to oblige.

48

Logan kicked off her shoes and headed into the kitchen. Shopping was exhausting. And they hadn't even been successful in finding a wedding venue for Amy. The places they'd seen so far were either too expensive or too elitist for Amy and Liam's taste. Amy was fine with getting married on the beach, but they needed a permit and there wasn't any parking. She wouldn't be surprised if they decided to elope.

She sighed. This was turning out to be a tougher job than she'd expected. Making her tried-and-true roast chicken for Solange was at least something she knew would turn out right. She set the oven to preheat at 425.

Generously slathering the chicken in butter, stuffing it with cut lemons and sprigs of fresh rosemary, Logan popped it into the narrow oven and went upstairs to shower. She hadn't had time to do much laundry lately but found a pair of linen pants she'd worn running the other day and a sleeveless white blouse to go with. Letting her hair down from a scrunchie, she finger combed it away from her face and loose around her shoulders and wiped the steam off the bathroom mirror. The sun had dusted her nose, cheeks, and shoulders with freckles and burnished her natural waves with glints of copper. A dusting of bronzer and some lip gloss made her green eyes pop. She was good to go.

Refreshed and dressed, she padded into the kitchen. The savory aroma enveloped her and made her mouth water. Opening the oven door a few inches, she peeked inside. Skin was crisping up nicely and smelled heavenly.

"Parfait!" she said, channeling her foreign-exchange mother who had given her the recipe.

She hoped Solange was a light eater.

Before leaving for work, Ben brought over his latest creation, a heat-and-leak-proof food basket that fit on the floorboard of Lola's passenger seat. Attractive and functional.

As promised, he also "threw in a few things" to round out the meal. She already had a green salad and fresh baguette from Tava'e's, but Ben extended the menu with an hors d'oeuvres of water crackers, black-olive-and-anchovy tapenade, and a fresh summer dessert of strawberry shortcake, homemade with real whipped cream.

The man was a god.

Per Solange's instructions, she did not add wine to the basket, looking forward to sampling a bottle from the French woman's cellar.

Avoiding the afternoon tangle on PCH, Logan made Lola climb Killer Hill and turn right, going through town slowly, but steadily, on Jacaranda Avenue, which ran a few blocks up and parallel to the beach. Not as scenic, but it would get her there faster. She wanted the chicken to still be hot, and the whipped cream cold, when she arrived. She had to make one stop on the way, to drop off the last of her grant applications at the post office, which was about six blocks away, before coming back to Solange's.

The short drive gave her time to reflect on the last couple of weeks. The attacks, Jeff's death, almost losing Amy in the storm. Almost losing Otter 1.

The funerals, Amy's engagement and upcoming wedding, the whole Fractals situation. She was still dealing with that last one. The family had decided. Their attorney called this morning to inform her they would not be funding any of their mother's former projects. Period. She didn't even have Rita's job offer to fall back on. She was sure it would be snapped up quickly.

Greuger said he was going to talk with the rest of the board to get them to finance at least Logan's salary for the first few months of the school year, until she could secure additional funding, but he didn't hold out much hope. Her old nemesis, Bitterman, still had friends at district, and they were friends with several board members. Instead of expanding Fractals, she might be shutting it down completely.

In the meantime, Amy was getting a lot of pressure from Liam's parents to "do things properly" in regards to their wedding, which, according to Liam's mother, meant spending more money and inviting half of Scotland. Logan hoped, for Amy's sake, that Liam had a backbone and stood up to his parents. It was their wedding. The way he handled this would tell Amy a lot about her future husband.

Last Monday, when Ben was working late, she'd indulged herself with a beach run, which cleared her mind, but she hadn't been out since.

She used to run whenever she wanted. It wasn't that Ben asked her stop. So why had she? She knew he'd be fine with her doing whatever, whenever. But he did like her to be home when he was home.

Jack had, too. Jack was a lot more obvious about it and pouted if she ever did something by herself or with a friend, so she'd gradually adjusted herself to his schedule. She didn't want that to happen with Ben. She didn't want to go backward. She wanted to be with someone, but still be herself.

Why did relationships have to be so hard?

Since she was just dropping off, she didn't have to wait in line at the post office. Now all she had to do was remember the name of the street to turn right on to get to Solange's place. Located on a bluff overlooking most of Jasper, it wasn't far, but the entrance to her property was way up the hill and wound around from the back.

Agate. That's it.

Recently tuned by Mr. Delgado, Logan's best friend's father and the best mechanic in the area, Lola made the steep climb without so much as a hiccup.

Approaching the driveway, Logan was glad they caught the man who had attacked Solange, killed Jeff, and almost got Amy. She shuddered at how close she came to losing her daughter.

According to Rick, the police hadn't caught him so much as found him already dead somewhere down in Guadalajara, Mexico. Through the driver's license picture Detective Andrews showed her, Solange identified the guy, an attorney named Schofield, as her attacker, but that's about all Rick knew. It was an ongoing investigation. If the detectives knew more, they weren't sharing.

Amy hadn't seen the attack on Jeff, but given that a man had tried to assault her just after Jeff was killed, they had to assume the attorney was not only Solange and Amy's attacker, but also the boy's murderer.

Logan was just glad it was over. Even though it was August, it wasn't too hot yet. She had a couple of weeks left to fund

Fractals or start looking for a job. Amy was happy and in love. And she had to admit, so was she.

She let that thought roll around in her mind.

She pulled in next to a black Ford F-150 that was parked beside Solange's silver Mercedes.

Must have company.

Logan parked and walked around to retrieve the food basket from the passenger side.

Down the bluff, the ocean sparkled, and the sky was denim blue. What a gorgeous view. Like Bonnie said . . . if no one was in jail or in the hospital, it was a good day.

Hooking the basket over her left forearm like Little Red Riding Hood, she knocked on the door of Grandma's house.

49

MONDAY, AUGUST 3, 2015

"I don't ask twice, and I don't take no for an answer," the man said calmly, waving Logan over to the couch with a gun. At least she thought it was a gun. She was too scared to look at it directly. Something dark gray and shiny was pointing at her. He'd already relieved her of her food basket at the door.

"Sit," he said.

She sat.

While he checked the windows for any other unwanted visitors, Logan tried to focus. Rick said something once he'd learned in the police academy about how to accurately describe someone. Something about estimating height to door frames and looking for details like are their earlobes attached or not.

This guy's head came up to the painting on the wall beside him. Large brown eyes, neat nails. Gold chain bracelet. Thick gold wedding ring. Hispanic. Solid, but not cut, dressed conservatively for a criminal. Nice jeans, golf shirt. Expensive-looking watch. Also gold.

If only she had known Solange's thin, raspy invitation to come in had been done at gunpoint.

"As soon as my business is attended to, I'll be out of your hair," the man stated calmly.

Logan was not reassured. She'd seen his face. She could identify him. Wasn't that always a bad sign? Didn't that mean they weren't planning on letting you live long enough to tell the police?

Think, Logan, think!

Solange sat very still, perched on the end of the couch, looking pale.

Just then, a Siamese cat stalked past the gunman and meowed at the sliding glass door leading onto the back patio.

"He wants out," Solange said.

The cat meowed again, this time pacing insistently back and forth.

The man nodded for Solange to open the door and let the cat out. She left it open.

"He'll be back in a few minutes," she said by way of explanation.

Continuing smoothly, as if the interruption hadn't occurred, the man went on. "As you may have heard," he said, directing his comment to Solange, "I no longer have an attorney, but scum suckers are easy to replace." His voice was smooth and low, almost honeyed. "I bought a new one last week and had these drawn up yesterday." He indicated the papers on the coffee table in front of them. Keeping the gun on Logan, he turned his head slightly left to Solange. "As we were discussing before your friend got here, all you need to do is sign."

Solange's hand wavered, and it looked like she might be sick. She dropped the pen.

"Now," he said.

Picking the pen back up, gripping it harder this time, she did.

"All three copies, *puta*," he said, never raising his voice.

When she was done, he had Logan place the original and all the copies into a secure messenger envelope and hand it to him. He tucked it under his arm.

Solange sank back against the cushions.

Not ready to leave yet, apparently, he took a moment to gloat.

Assuming he was going to kill them, Logan looked for an opening—any opening. If she could knock the gun out of his hand, maybe it would go off and a neighbor would hear it and call the cops. Or better yet, come help.

Right. Nobody in their right mind would run into a house where they'd heard gunshots.

It wasn't much of a plan, but there was no time to make a better one.

The man seemed more relaxed now. He'd gotten what he came for and seemed in no rush to leave.

"Allow me to introduce myself, Mrs. McKenna. Felix Rodriguez."

It was not a good sign he knew her name.

"Yes, I know all of you people. All you otter people," he laughed.

He sat down in one of the chairs but kept the gun trained at Logan's chest. She hoped he knew how to handle that thing, and it wouldn't go off accidentally, then realized that was a weird thing to wish. She probably shouldn't want her attacker to be an experienced gunman.

"You know what this is about, don't you?"

"No," she said honestly.

"Money," he said. "Just money. And hard work. But not

necessarily my own." He stretched his legs out in front of him, then pulled them back, resting his elbows on his knees. "My father now, and his father, and every other wetback father, brother, or uncle. They worked hard. Gardening. Pounding nails. Eking out a living. But they don't get a very big piece of the pie. Just a little slice. And they're supposed to say thank you, then crawl back across the border when they're done. But me, I figured it out. You don't settle for a sliver and you don't say thank you. You take the whole pie."

None of this made any sense to Logan, but she wasn't in a position to ask questions. The longer he rambled, the longer they stayed alive.

"This land, for example," he tapped the messenger envelope. "Lot 429. Thanks to your generous gift just now, I own the surface of it. But thanks to the greed of my former attorney, I also own its guts. All the riches underneath—that big pool of oil just sitting there, waiting to be sucked out. There's a *fortune* under there. But I don't have to get it out. I don't have to do the work. I just have to sell it to someone who will." He leaned back and smiled broadly. "*And* I own a controlling share of your idiot half brother's project, Paradise Shores. Isn't he going to be surprised when he finds out the oil company's going to drill right under him? Even if he wins in court, he loses."

Logan felt sorry for Scott but was relieved to learn he wasn't part of this. That would have crushed Solange. She heard Scott had visited his new sister several times in the hospital.

"Well, I'd love to stay, but I have several phone calls to make on the drive back," Felix said, "and you're coming with, Ms. McKenna."

He made them both stand up, put Logan in front of him, then turned and casually backhanded Solange hard across the face, knocking her back toward the couch.

Someone rang the doorbell.

Was everyone visiting Solange today?

Felix tightened his grip on Logan and stuck the muzzle of his gun between her shoulder blades.

"Not one sound," he whispered into her ear.

She had no intention of making any sound, let alone more than one.

Not daring to move her head, she cut her eyes back over to the couch, where Solange was slumped sideways, half-on, half-off the couch. She hoped she was okay. The woman was in her seventies. How many hits could she take? She was just recovering from being strangled.

"Ms. Sauvage?" said the voice from outside. "It's Detective Diaz. My partner spoke with you on the phone. We have an appointment to speak with you today. We need you to review and sign your statement. " He knocked again. "Ms. Sauvage? Are you there?"

Held against his chest, but not as tightly now, Logan heard Felix's shallow breaths and felt his sweat through the back of her shirt. Trying to hold herself perfectly still, her right calf was beginning to cramp.

Hoping Felix was too distracted to notice, she very carefully bent her right wrist and slowly extracted a small canister of pepper spray from her pocket.

Thank you, Little Brother.

He'd been insisting she carry pepper spray on her runs. Just as she was gathering her courage, planning her GI Jane attack, she felt as much as saw a shadow darkening the back door Solange had left open for the cat. Felix turned to look over his right shoulder, moving his gun away from her as he did so.

It was now or never.

Logan whipped around, tried to hold the can as far from her own face as possible, squeezed her eyes shut, and aimed.

At the same time, she heard someone rushing in from the open door behind them, yelling, "Police! Drop the gun! Drop the gun!"

Felix got slammed into the wall just as she pressed the top of the can down, letting loose a powerful stream of pepper spray . . .

. . . right into the eyes of her rescuer, Detective Andrews.

While Andrews and Solange were being treated by the EMTs, Diaz cuffed Felix and pushed him into the back of one of the squad cars recently arrived on the scene to take him into the station.

Miraculously, Solange was okay.

"We French have very hard heads," she said, refusing to return to the hospital.

"I am perfectly fine," she insisted. "I do not wish to leave my home."

With a promise she would call someone to come stay with her for the night, they finally relented and packed up their gear.

After giving yet another police statement, Logan was also released. She put the chicken in the fridge and shared a glass of the wonderful Domaine aux Moines Savennieres Solange had intended for their meal, while waiting for her babysitter to arrive.

Logan learned that she and Scott were pulling the case out of court. They weren't sure how yet, but they were going to sort out the lot 429 issues equitably. One thing both were set on—the Southern Sea Otter Sanctuary and Education Center would open on schedule. Apparently, Scott had met Sadie— everyone had given up calling her Otter 1—and it was love at first sight. Solange filling the dual roles of sister and mother figure didn't hurt, either.

What Felix and Gary hadn't known was that the California state legislature was passing a bill protecting wildlife centers from having any minerals extracted from the property if it disturbed the animals. And drilling for oil would definitely disturb recovering sea otters.

Everything else could be worked out. Solange was having a proper will drawn up, leaving everything to Scott, which went a long way toward helping him give up his Pacific Shores project on lot 429. In the meantime, they had already started working on a creative and profitable project on another piece of Solange's property in Cormorant Canyon. Scott was building an even better version of his dream project, while also establishing a much-needed wildlife corridor.

According to Tava'e, who overheard their planning sessions when they met at her coffee shop, brother and sister continued to argue about the balance between the needs of animals and people, but at least they did it over decent meals.

They were family.

Although he would have to stay out of Detective Andrews's way for a while, Rick was proud of his big sister. He and Paula promptly bought her another can of pepper spray.

Amy and Liam came by to make sure she was all right, and Ben didn't let Logan out of his sight for several days.

Home never felt better.

50

Digging her toes down into the cool, wet sand, Logan looked out to sea, watching the lazy orange ball that was the sun slip past the horizon into the sea.

On Bonnie's insistence, she bought, and actually wore, heels to go with her dress, but kicked them off as soon as the ceremony was over. What was the purpose of having a beach wedding if you couldn't go barefoot? She refused to buy a frumpy beige mother-of-the-bride outfit, so with Amy's permission, she had ordered a simple sea-green sundress online. It worked perfectly.

A soft breeze lifted her hair off her shoulders. From here, she could hear the band and see the glow of garden lights strung across the wooden dance floor, illuminating the happy, swirling wedding guests. She'd go back in a minute, but for now, she relished this moment.

Everything had gone beautifully. Somehow they'd managed to please Liam's very particular parents, who'd flown in from

Scotland a week ago, ready to take over, only to find everything handled.

Logan bought Amy's dress, and she and Ben gave the newlyweds something toward their honeymoon. Luckily, that's all the help they needed, because she was just about at the last of her savings. The board had spoken. She had until the thirtieth to find the funding for Fractals or she was unemployed. Again.

Amy's dress was perfect, though. Four days before the wedding, they decided to try the '70s place down the hill. They discovered a vintage ivory lace dream, carefully folded and layered in tissue in the bottom drawer of a handsome bow dresser, obtained by the owner of the shop in an estate sale. The original bride had been a little bustier than Amy, but with Bonnie's sewing skills, the dress was converted into an elegant strapless wedding gown that fit Amy as if it had been designed for her.

Wanting everything "done right" for their only son, Liam's mother originally wished to hold the reception at the prestigious Pacific Newport Golf Club, where, she informed them, "We have reciprocal privileges with our club in Scotland." But after seeing Tava'e's oceanfront spread, she wisely kept her mouth shut.

She also wanted a large, traditional wedding at a proper church, with a guest list long enough for "your father's extensive business associates" and every relative, no matter how distant, who could be counted on for a gift.

They reached a compromise. Announcements were sent to everyone, but Liam put his foot down, and the wedding was kept to a manageable size. The boy had a backbone after all.

Tava'e insisted on taking charge of the food, as well as providing the venue. Her and Jean's gift to the new couple. Until she drove Amy there to look at it, Logan had never seen their home.

DEVIL'S CLAW

When Tava'e walked them through the living room to get to the backyard, Amy's jaw dropped and her eyes grew wide. Koa-wood floors topped with natural fiber rugs, stretched to a wall of windows overlooking a dramatic ocean view.

OMG! Amy mouthed silently to her mom.

When they stepped out onto the stretch of white, sandy beach where the ceremony and reception were going to be, she started jumping up and down. Squealing, she gave the Samoan woman a huge hug.

"Thank you! Thank you! This is so perfect!" Amy said.

With a thousand relatives to get the work done, Tava'e didn't need much help from them, so Amy and Logan spent much of the next two weeks at the center with Sadie and Otter 2. Gina had given up on ever releasing Sadie back to the wild, so Amy's otter became the first permanent resident of the center and official children's ambassador.

Otter 2, the rescued male pup from La Jolla, was working with a surrogate mother on loan from the Monterey Bay Aquarium. They'd forgiven Gina for jumping the gun and were fully supporting her efforts. Otter 2 was scheduled to be released in a couple of months if all continued to go well with his training. Gina made sure everyone working with *this* otter wore their gear and went by the rules. But secretly, Gina had named him Jeff.

Ben had his guys put the final touches on the new tile work and hooked up the sculpture fountain Solange had designed. The opening of the center was a huge success. They were already booked for class field trips through November.

Guests began arriving at Tava'e's around 6:00 p.m.

Amy asked Ben to give her away, and for the wedding march, she asked her mom to play a lilting Scottish tune to walk her down the plumeria-strewn, sandy aisle, where Liam waited, beaming.

The simple ceremony was over by seven. Everyone carried their folding chairs back up to the tables and got ready to eat. The smell of dinner had been driving everyone crazy for the last half hour.

Jean outdid himself. Baskets of fresh, aromatic French bread filled the tables. The spread started with trays of delicate prosciutto-wrapped asparagus; ruby-red sliced tomatoes topped with fresh mozzarella and basil, drizzled in olive oil; and tossed green salad. Herbed olive oil or butter for the bread. Ratatouille for the vegetarians, bacon-wrapped scallops, shrimp, and, for the true carnivores, Tava'e's relatives roasted a pig in the traditional Samoan umu style. And of course, tons of steaming white rice. It was all delicious.

Danny and Epiphany manned the coffee bar and dessert table, which boasted a towering coconut wedding cake. For the chocoholics like Logan, there was molten lava sauce, otherwise known as hot fudge, and ice cream on the side. Or poured all over the coconut cake, whichever you preferred.

"Hey, beautiful," Ben said, wrapping his arms around her.

Rubbing her arms up and down to warm them, he gave her his jacket and spread a blanket he'd spirited out of the trunk of his car. Pulling her against him, he wrapped her in his arms.

Leaning back, she smiled up at him. Blue eyes, spilling over with emotion, burned into her green ones.

This man loved her. This beautiful, good man loved her. How had she gotten so lucky? A lump rose in her throat, and tears threatened to fall onto her own cheeks.

For the next few minutes, until the cold chased them back to the warmth of the crowd, they sat wrapped in each other's arms, watching the moon play over the water.

Epilogue

Logan sat in her office over the former garage and looked out the windows. Amy and Liam were off on their honeymoon. The man who'd attacked Solange, chased Amy into an angry ocean, and killed Jeff, had been killed himself.

And the man who'd held her at gunpoint and coldly dispatched Solange with a hard blow to the head, Felix Rodriguez, was in custody, awaiting trial. The man had been so overconfident, he hadn't bothered covering his tracks. Rick said Detective Andrews had a ton of evidence against him. The normally careful criminal had operated so long under the radar he thought he was immune to detection. Blinded by greed, Felix Rodriguez was going away for a very long time.

The sun was up, but the day lay before her, coated in a thin gray film. She felt an urge to get up and scrub the whites white again—make the colors pop.

She sighed and brought her attention back inside. She'd done everything she could, but she was going to have to face facts. Only a few small grants had come through. Not enough to save Fractals. Or her job.

She might as well make the calls. School started in five days.

That wouldn't give Tilly and Jeremy much time to go back to regular teaching again and set up their classrooms or prepare lessons for the first week of school, but she'd help, and Ben said he'd pitch in over Labor Day weekend. It was the least she could do.

She was grateful they didn't have to outright fire anyone. They would still have jobs. Being only temporarily assigned to Fractals, they were still on contract with the district. There were always a few openings at the beginning of the year due to unexpected changes in enrollment or teachers extending maternity leave. But they would have no control over their assignment. They'd be placed wherever there was an opening— and right now, the only posts on the job board were in primary K–3. Tilly Jones was an accomplished jazz pianist, and Jeremy Allen a talented saxophonist and popular middle school band leader. She couldn't picture either one of them teaching the Hokey Pokey to kindergarteners. She couldn't put it off any longer. Logan reached for her phone.

She chickened out and dialed Jeremy's number first. He was less scary than Tilly. Before he answered, call waiting beeped through. Happy to put off her conversation with Jeremy another five minutes, she took the call.

"Logan! Glad you were in. Rita here," the familiar voice said. "How do you feel about commuting?"

"Commuting?"

That didn't make any sense. She couldn't fly back and forth to the New School to teach math and music. What was she talking about?

When Rita offered her the job originally, Logan was tempted, but had turned it down. She hadn't turned it down just to keep Fractals alive. Although she loved everything Rita was doing at the New School, with Ben in her life, and hopefully even Amy and Liam nearby, she didn't want to move.

But now she was out of a job, so she decided to hear her out.

What Rita had to offer was better than a job.

Not one to allow talent to slip through her fingers, Rita had funneled some of her own grant money, with permission from her own benefactors, of course, to expand Fractals in size and scope. Sort of a dual-campus proposition.

She told Logan she could add the technical and programming expertise of Huey, including his animated dolphin computer program, and all Logan had to do was promise to help hire people to replicate the existing music/math courses at the New School campus.

As far as commuting, Logan would only need to commit to going up there a few weeks up front, while they hired the new staff, and visits as needed after that. Rita estimated that after the initial setup, no more than twenty percent of her year would need to be spent physically up at the New School. There was money for Huey to come to California and train her people here.

If Logan was interested, Rita would fly down next week and work out the details.

Logan shut her eyes and held her breath, trying to think. The woman had turned herself inside out to make this happen. She deserved an answer.

Fractals could keep going. Tilly and Jeremy would get to keep doing what they loved. She got Huey! He was amazing. Her brain was already buzzing with ways they could integrate technology into the program.

But best of all, she didn't have to give up the life she had just begun to build. Gazing out at the ocean from her rooftop deck. With Ben.

Suddenly, things became very clear.

"Yes," she said, feeling a flood of relief. "Hell yes!"

ACKNOWLEDGMENTS

I would like to thank the following people for giving generously of their time and expertise as I researched the wide-ranging topics for this book. They patiently answered my many questions and helped me to begin to understand the complicated and often layered and overlapping environmental, probate, and land-use laws.

I had the pleasure of spending quite a bit of time with Michelle Sousa, assistant curator of mammals and birds at the Aquarium of the Pacific in Long Beach. After more than twenty years of experience working with southern sea otters, she loves the little guys, and she gave me one of Gina's lines in the book, that she'd never turn her back on a sea otter. "They are unpredictable, wild animals. You can be rubbing their tummy one minute; the next, the claws come out and they're attacking your arm." Good to keep in mind if a friendly sea otter ever approaches your kayak and wants to play.

Ron Eby and Robert Scoles gave me a glimpse into their experiences as citizen scientists. They lead the Elkhorn Slough Reserve's otter efforts. Tim Tinker is the lead scientist on this NOAA and Fish "and Wildlife project, which is in its fourth year as of 2017.

Laird Henkel, senior environmental scientist supervisor of the Marine Wildlife Veterinary Care and Research Center, is in charge of the Office of Spill Prevention and Response for the California Department of Fish and Wildlife in Santa Cruz. Laird provided invaluable descriptions of what setting up a sea otter sanctuary would involve and what elements it would need to have. Who knew that Dawn dishwashing soap was the best thing they've found yet to get oil out of otter fur? To accommodate the story, I took some liberties with the laws involving sending all sick sea otters to Monterey Bay Aquarium but stuck with the facts as much as possible.

Professor Joseph DiMento, UC Irvine School of Law, took the time to put me in touch with several experts, and an estate-planning lawyer, Ethan Miller-Basemore, gave insight into trust litigation, a specialty of his, which helped me craft a plausible, equally strong claim for two of my characters on a piece of property each believes they own independently. The details involved brother/sister DNA, handwriting analysis, holographic wills, how much such a battle might cost both parties, and where and how it may be waged.

As always, I am grateful to my editor, Laura Petrella, for polishing my scribbles into a legible manuscript I can deliver to my publisher. Everyone's hard work is much appreciated. Believe me, writing is only half the battle when birthing a book.

Many thanks go to Kim Peticolas for bringing these new editions of the Logan series to life. Her powerful cover designs and sleek interiors are awesome!

Finally, I want to thank my husband, John, for his unfailing love and support. And that goes for all my family and friends. No woman is an island.

If I have forgotten anyone, please forgive me, and as always, the expertise is theirs, all remaining errors are mine.

ABOUT THE AUTHOR

A self-admitted book addict, Valerie Davisson was the kid with the flashlight under her pillow, reading long after lights out. After a life of travel, she now lives on the Oregon coast with her husband, John, and their new puppy, Finn. When not working on her latest book, she's probably in the kitchen, cooking up a storm for family and friends.

Enjoyed the Book?

If you enjoyed this book, please consider leaving a review on Amazon or Goodreads. And be sure to check out the rest of the Logan McKenna series.

> Shattered (Book 1)
> Forest Park (Book 2)
> Vanishing Day (Book 4)

Want to know more about Valerie Davisson or her next book? Make sure to visit www.valeriedavisson.com and sign up for her newsletter.